Jill Roe

In 1993 Jill Roe was the winner of a writing competition run by the *Mail on Sunday* and this encouraged her to write seriously. Born in West Cornwall, she now lives in Somerset with her husband. Her previous four novels, *Angels Flying Slowly*, *A New Leaf*, *The Topiary Garden* and *A Well Kept Secret* are also available from Sceptre.

SCEPTRE

Eating Grapes
Downwards

Jill Roe

SCEPTRE

First published in 1999 by Hodder and Stoughton
First published in paperback in 2000 by Hodder and Stoughton
A division of Hodder Headline
A Sceptre Paperback

A CIP catalogue record for this book is
available from the British Library.

ISBN 0 340 68281 7

Printed and bound in Great Britain by
Mackays of Chatham PLC, Chatham, Kent

Hodder and Stoughton
A division of Hodder Headline
338 Euston Road
London NW1 3BH

For Malcolm with love

1972

⬥⬥⬥⬥⬥⬥⬥⬥⬥

'Who's this one of?' Violet Jarvie handed a photograph to her mother. Dorcas took it from Violet's hand, surprised to see that the image was translating into sepia so that the feet of the three girls pictured together in the foreground appeared to be wreathed in smoke. 'I can recognise you but who're the others?'

Dorcas looked at the photograph for a long time before she said, 'That was taken on your father's twenty-first birthday. I'm in the middle and the other two were my best friends, Lally and Gerry.'

'Lally?'

'Mary Marigold Bassett. She had a sort of nanny to look after her who couldn't pronounce her Rs so Mary Marigold came out sounding like Lally, almost as if Effie had been Chinese.'

'And Gerry? Is she that dotty old cousin of Daddy's?'

'Not dotty and not old but, yes, a cousin of your father's. We all had a joint birthday party that year and this was taken just before Daddy drove the three of us from Petty Place where I lived to this house in his old Austin 10. Look you can just see the palm trees in the background in Granny Alma's garden.'

In the photograph Dorcas saw again the ribbons tied to the Austin as if it were a bridal car, the cowslips bunched and secured to the bonnet and she felt the excitement as she and Lally and Gerry had squeezed into the green leather seats pretending to be anxious that their party frocks would be crushed, their shoes muddied by the path along which they had walked.

Dorcas returned the fading picture to the shoe box which Violet, the middle one of her children, bored and nursing a broken collar-bone, was pretending to sort. She remembered the shoes she had worn that night; low heeled satin dyed a green the colour of ivy leaves to match the green-and-blue plaid of her dress. Neither she nor Gerry would really have cared if their feet had become dusty as they hurried to Eugene's car but Lally would have minded. Oh yes, Lally would certainly have minded.

CHAPTER ONE

1947

———◆◆◆———

Dorcas Westley could never remember precisely her first meeting with Lally Bassett, as every encounter became fused with many others, each one filled with anticipation, which commuted as the visit progressed to a sense of disbelief and alarm.

From the time that she could understand at all Dorcas was under no illusion about the reason for her visits to the Bassetts: she was expected to behave acceptably, to answer politely when spoken to, to comply with whatever Aunt Coral said and to be generally amenable to whatever was suggested. Above all she was to make herself agreeable to Lally Bassett, for it was undoubtedly Lally who would decide whether or not Dorcas would be welcome at the house in Advent Gardens.

'The most desirable property in the most select area of Penalverne,' Lally had said to Dorcas when they were ten and lying in the hot grass which was allowed to grow long around the garden shed which Aunt Coral called 'the Wendy house'. The air was thick with pollen from dispersing seed heads, dry as firewood, golden and fragrant as hay. Dorcas wanted to be left alone to read but Lally had decided to talk and where Lally led, Dorcas was expected to follow.

Dorcas let the book slip through her fingers until it rested on her chest but she closed her eyes so that compliance with Lally had to be assumed. She could smell the creosote that Uncle Billy Bassett had used to treat the wood of the shed, the reek of smoked bacon, acrid as the tar on the road menders' cart that enveloped Dorcas on her walk from Dobells Path to Advent Gardens. All her life the smell of sun on creosote would remind Dorcas of Lally; fragile, freckled legs stretched out in front of her, hair like unravelled twine caught back in two pink, bow-shaped slides. Even then it seemed that there was something unfinished about Lally Bassett: her hair seemed to lack conventional colour and her eyes, fringed with almost white lashes, were so pale that they seemed like water, white or grey or blue, never quite as you remembered them, disconcerting in their inconstancy.

When Dorcas had repeated Lally's remark to her mother, Alma Westley had laughed. 'I suppose she got that from Coral. She fills that child's head with so much nonsense it's no wonder Lally's such an odd little creature.' Alma was shaping dumplings and Dorcas could already imagine the slimy outer layer of dough sticking to her teeth as she watched her mother's square, small hands working swiftly and methodically to prepare a stew that would cook unattended while she was at work.

Dorcas was practised at judging the moment when her mother was most receptive, when she could make her feel guilty about having to leave her only child alone in the house in Dobells Path. 'If Lally is an odd little creature why do I have to go there all the time?'

'Don't start that again, Dorcas, *please*; you know I have to work.' Alma Westley dried her hands on the roller towel behind the kitchen door. She looked at Dorcas and sat down lightly on a high stool, almost perched, as if for instant flight. 'Dorcas, listen to me.' Alma reached for her daughter's hand. 'Don't ever repeat what I say about Lally, will you? She's just a bit unusual, that's all – I shouldn't have said that she's odd. Coral's very kind and without her help I don't know how we'd manage. I can't afford to pay her very much and I couldn't work at all if she hadn't offered to look after you sometimes.'

'I didn't know you paid her.' Dorcas felt diminished, unsettled by this new, uncalled-for knowledge.

Alma looked at her daughter: Coral's request for a weekly sum to cover what she called 'her outgoings over Dorcas' had come as a blow, Alma having felt certain that Coral's offer had been made out of friendship. 'It's not very much and Coral does feed you sometimes . . .'

'Her food's disgusting and I have to eat Lally's leftovers. Do you know what I had yesterday?' Alma shook her head, fearful of revealing to Dorcas the indignation she tried so hard to commute to gratitude towards Coral. 'It was *liver sandwiches*. I thought I was going to be sick *and* she makes me say grace. Can't you talk to her, Mum?'

'I'll try, my bird, I will try.'

'Daddy used to call me his bird.'

'I know.' Alma's eyes filled with tears as she thought of Roy lying cold and lonely in the ugly, pale coffin that was all she had been able to afford. When the rain blew horizontally off the sea and the fronds of the palm tree in her tiny front garden swayed and parted like long hair in the wind, Alma wished that she had defied his family and had insisted that Roy be cremated, the thought of him lying alone in the heavy wet earth almost more than she could bear.

Roy's mother and his sisters had stood together, segregated and dry eyed around the family plot, while Alma and Dorcas wept as he was lowered down the artificial grass bank into the darkness and damp of his grave. After the funeral the Westleys, with a deliberate show of reluctance, had accepted tea and fruit cake from Alma and had placed dry, brittle kisses lightly on Dorcas's cheek as they left. Apart from a card and a postal order for five shillings on her birthday and at Christmas, which Dorcas dutifully acknowledged, there was minimal communication from Roy's family and Alma was too proud to ask for help.

She knew they wouldn't understand that the poverty which lapped at the edges of her life with a child to look after was of Roy's making and she felt sure they would condemn her as profligate. 'Always had big ideas, that one,' she could almost hear them saying, never for a moment acknowledging that it was their son and brother who had gambled with what small security his wife and child might have been expected to enjoy. Far from providing inappropriate luxuries, Alma needed to earn money to provide those necessities which hid their penury from the world: shoes for Dorcas; clothes as she grew taller and broad; even food sometimes when Roy had been having a run of worse than usual luck.

Alma had just begun to question the practicality of staying with a man whose only assets were charm and a certain helplessness, when Roy Westley had collapsed on a zebra crossing, his wallet full of money for the first time in many months. When his belongings were restored to Alma there had been nothing more than the 6s 10d he had in his pocket and she had accepted this as being exactly what she would have expected, paying the milkman's bill with her husband's inadequate legacy. In spite of the difficulties inherent in being married to a man with an incurable weakness, Alma had loved her husband and she and Dorcas missed him still, their family now manifestly incomplete.

Dorcas remembered her grandmother, after whom she had been named, as hatted, grey gloved and indifferent to human weakness. When Mrs Westley took off her hat indoors she immediately put on an enveloping floral apron and for a long time the small Dorcas had assumed that one action was consequent upon the other.

With her two elderly daughters Mrs Westley had watched her son's widow from a distance and had found it easy to deny acknowledgement of the anxiety which Alma hid by gaiety and insouciance as she tackled one unsatisfactory job after another. It had been Coral Bassett who had caught Alma Westley as the waters of debt and desperation threatened to engulf her altogether.

Coral Paice and Alma Sidney had been at school together not, as Coral now told people, 'in Penalverne', allowing them to draw the conclusion that she had been at St Catherine's, but at the Council School at the wrong end of town, up near the Recreation Ground where the houses jostled together, row upon row of granite terraces with a yard at the back and an even smaller yard at the front. Here and there a hedge denied immediate access to the rooms below the level of the pavement. There were steps down to these lower rooms with their wide, enlightening windows, and most were shielded from the intrusion of strangers' passing gaze only by a set of railings and an iron gate set in incongruous granite pillars. It was here that Alma Sidney had felt at home and where Coral Paice knew herself to be held in only temporary captivity.

The room glimpsed by passers-by from the pavement was where most people discharged their daily lives, not in the upper part of the house with its stiff, frost-white curtains and muffled scales practised on an upright piano by fingers clumsy with cold and lack of ability.

Life in the rooms upstairs was restricted, circumscribed by the necessities of politeness or the obligation of distress, and it was downstairs, secure in the certainty of their acceptance, that joy and sorrow were expressed unconcealed. Here tea was dispensed accompanied by arcane advice; where secret medicines changed hands and recipes were exchanged more openly; where gossip magnified to become truth, and truth was overlaid with enough kindness to allow it to become tolerable.

Alma Sidney and Coral Paice had grown up together in this autonomous, conspiratorial world of adult mystery and children's submission. As they grew older each regarded the other as an impediment from which there seemed to be no escape. Coral, always just too plump and with a face which seemed to have no underlying structure was, nevertheless, considered to be good looking although her several small attractions never quite amounted to true beauty. Nevertheless she made the most of what she had; her hands were small and elegant and she took good care of her nails. Her ankles were neat and she wore good shoes to distract the eye from legs that were shorter than she would have liked, and much sturdier. It was Coral's hair, though, that attracted attention wherever she went: it was long and thick and the colour of old copper and had a lustrous sheen enhanced by the simplicity of a style that showed off its unusual beauty to the greatest advantage – an artifice of which Coral was well aware.

Alma was no prettier than Coral but she had a vivacity about her that attracted people in a way that Coral's restraint never did. There was something too calculated in Coral's reserve – too obvious and implacable her ambition to leave Gwavas Terrace – that inhibited casual friendships. The attention that Coral attracted was usually from men who joked that *still waters run deep*. They were swiftly repulsed for Coral Paice was not interested in minnows. She had found herself a job as typist in a bank and had, by diligence and attention to detail, learned a great deal about the distribution of money in Penalverne and was content to wait until a suitably big fish was lured towards her opportunely spread net. It was Billy Bassett, third son of the Bassetts of Reskadinnick, who rose to Coral's spinner, not noticing until it was too late the hook it concealed. Coral appeared compliant and accomplished to Billy, and he seemed unaware that the attraction he felt towards his new wife was a reflection of the affection he had felt years before for a nurserymaid whom he had shared with his brothers.

The connection was not lost on Billy's mother but Judith Bassett, the most realistic of women, saw that Coral Paice had both determination and tenacity – hadn't she, after all, lured Billy away from a putative fiancée when their engagement was all but official? Billy was amiable and good natured but not even his mother could truthfully say that he was other than indolent, and Mrs Bassett had to admit that Coral Paice would make him a good wife. In time she came to tolerate Coral but never, even after many years, could it be said that she came near to liking her.

Coral was aware of the antipathy of Billy's family towards her but she had expected it, sure that when they grew to appreciate her their resistance would disappear. It was one calculation in which Coral was mistaken: she had done everything that she could to make herself acceptable to the Bassetts but they never revised their opinion of Billy's unsuitable wife and over the years the distance between the Penalverne Bassetts and the rest of the family continued to widen.

Coral had made few genuine friends on her journey from Gwavas Terrace to Advent Gardens: she had watched and listened and had learned her lessons well but there was still a certain hesitancy, adroitly concealed, that marked her out as an intruder in the family into which she had married. It was a weakness which she was perceptive enough to acknowledge, determining that her only child would win the acceptance of all the Bassetts — that acceptance which had always evaded Coral herself.

Coral had endured two miscarriages before Lally was born and it was the birth of the small, delicate baby that gave Coral the ascendancy in her marriage that had so far eluded her. Judith Bassett arranged for a nurse to look after Coral and the baby for a few weeks when the fragile little girl was allowed home but with every sign of progress that the baby made it seemed as if strength for her daughter's advancement was depleting Coral's own reserves. Her energy and determination appeared to be expended on the effort of encouraging Mary Marigold to take a firm grasp on the existence which had so nearly cost both of them their lives.

Billy was afraid of the baby; of her precarious little breaths and the waxy paleness of her skin. He was more afraid of Nurse Maysmith, who called him 'Daddy' and who stood at his side as if to field the shawl-swaddled bundle should he, his size and clumsiness exaggerated, make a sideways pass forgetting it was his daughter he held and not a rugger ball. Billy was never hesitant in returning the baby to Nurse Maysmith's capable hands, thankful that he had done no damage and determined to protect Mary Marigold from the injury that he saw everywhere around her.

Billy Bassett loved his daughter with such passion that his eyes would fill with tears when he looked at her unprepared little features and the halo of white hair which, even then, seemed the most vital thing about her. He knew he could forgive Coral anything for persevering in her determination to give him the child who lay so lightly in the yellow decorated crib in the nursery.

Coral, astute and watchful as ever, saw that her daughter had been an investment whose value would increase as she grew older and that Mary Marigold had assured for her mother command of the balance of the marriage to Billy of which she had never been entirely certain. Coral felt none of the tenderness for their daughter that so affected Billy; none of his absurd pride in her conventional achievements and certainly none of his leniency in forgiving Mary Marigold her faults. Mary

Marigold's lapses from the standard of behaviour which Coral had set for her were few. Few, that is, that were apparent and none that was pronounced. Mary Marigold was a tranquil baby who grew into a child of such a visibly amenable disposition that she was welcomed everywhere by Coral's acquaintances and spent many hours sitting with a puzzle or stubby wax crayons, forgotten, or at least ignored, while Coral and her friends gossiped and drank or played an idle hand of cards. Occasionally someone would pass Mary Marigold a few marshmallows or a drink of barley water and say what a good little girl she was not to make herself a nuisance as so many other children did.

Once or twice on Effie Sweet's day off, Coral had left the child on her own in the kitchen with plasticine or a book of magic painting and while Mary Marigold drew the wet brush carefully inside the lines on the page, watching the pale pink-and-green wash transform fairies and flowers, Coral went to lie down, explaining to the little girl that she wasn't feeling terribly well and needed to be left on her own for a while.

On these occasions, when Effie returned, neither she nor Mary Marigold seemed to be aware that there was an unfamiliar smell of tobacco in the house and later on Coral would open the window in her bedroom and tell Mary Marigold to fetch the frosted blue glass atomiser which stood on the dressing-table. Mary Marigold was allowed to squeeze the rubber bulb from which hung a tangled silk tassel and she sniffed at the sweetness of Evening Gardenia which seeped around the other, unfamiliar, smells in the bedroom. Coral's headache always seemed to have lifted after one of these lie-downs and Coral had made Mary Marigold promise that she would never tell anyone, especially Daddy, that Mummy had such terrible headaches that she needed to rest in the afternoon. It would be their secret and Mary Marigold understood, didn't she, that it was a sin to break a promise?

If Mary Marigold's own contemporaries were less enthusiastic about her company than their parents appeared to be, their protests were overridden and Mary Marigold became a guest in most of the houses of a certain small section of Penalverne society, her presence tolerated rather than enjoyed by the children who should have been her friends.

Although Coral felt none of the surpassing love for her daughter with which Billy's life had been transformed, there was affection of a kind; approval appropriate to Mary Marigold's achievements. Coral had worked hard to eliminate from her own voice all trace of the local intonation and only, very occasionally when she was laughing with Effie, would she forget and speak as she had done when she lived in Gwavas Terrace. Mary Marigold was not to be allowed any lapse of this sort and Coral arranged for her to have private elocution lessons which, she explained to a bemused Billy, were only to build his daughter's confidence of talking in public. Mary Marigold's confidence was also to be built by piano lessons, ballet lessons, swimming and tennis lessons in the summer and riding lessons all the year round. Through it all Mary Marigold did as she was told, said very little and fell short in everything of achieving what Coral expected of her.

There was in Coral Bassett some vein of deceit apparent only to those people who disliked her but which seemed obscured from those to whom she was closest. Shortly after Mary Marigold's birth Billy had come home from work one day to find that the double divan he and Coral had previously shared had been replaced by twin beds. Billy was given to understand that it was for his good alone: he was all too aware that Coral had nearly died giving him a child and to avoid the possibility of a tragedy in the future it was better that they sleep apart for a little while.

The little while had stretched into years and Billy had grown used to his nightly solitude, accepting it as a penance, unwilling to inflict more pain on Coral when she already seemed to suffer so many trivial but debilitating illnesses. If Billy ever suspected that Coral's indispositions were due more to expediency than fact, he had only to look at Mary Marigold, the daughter whose very existence gave meaning to his life, and he would stifle whatever unsympathetic thoughts came into his mind and fetch Coral a cup of tea or some arrowroot biscuits, whatever might help her to recover more quickly.

The only person who was unaffected by Coral's moods was Effie Sweet, and Effie hardly counted. Effie

Sweet had been lent to her daughter-in-law by Judith Bassett when the monthly nurse had left and Coral had seemed disinclined, or unable, to look after the baby on her own.

Effie's position in the Bassett household had always been ambiguous. As a newly married woman Judith Bassett had been prevailed upon by Reverend Mother Gertrude to take Effie Sweet into her employ and if any resemblance at all between Effie and the family she looked after was noticed, no-one had ever dared to express the thought aloud. Effie called herself a companion, but to whom was debatable. She walked the dogs and took them to the vet; she sent parcels and newspaper cuttings from *The Universe* to the three Bassett boys when they were away at school, and over the years she had sewn on hundreds of name tapes and all, all, accompanied by chuckling and giggling, sometimes even an onslaught of merriment escaping in guffaws of laughter and excited song. Effie matched wool for Judith Bassett's *petit point*, took Terrance Bassett's shoes to be mended, and occasionally prepared the family's food which gave rise, Terrance Bassett had been heard to remark, to an understanding, by God, of the phrase, 'a good plain cook'. The years she had spent in the orphanage had not been wasted and Effie could darn and iron, wash china without chipping or dropping it, take cuttings from difficult plants, which always flourished, and was perpetually, insuppressibly cheerful.

It was this impervious, invincible cheerfulness which prompted Judith Bassett to offer Effie's services to Coral.

'Just for a little while,' Judith had said, 'until you're quite well again. Actually,' Judith was conspiratorial, 'now that it's just Terrance and me at home we don't *need* Effie so much and I know she'd absolutely *adore* to have a new baby to look after. Will you take her?' Coral had agreed and Effie Sweet had moved into what Coral called the maid's room at the house in Advent Gardens. If anyone suspected that Judith Bassett had acted out of anything other than altruism, they were sensible enough to keep the thought to themselves.

Effie reminded Coral of a Pekinese that had worried her as a child and Effie's difficulty in articulating certain words gave her speech a curious Chinese inflection which reinforced this impression. It was Effie, inevitably, who had been responsible for Mary Marigold becoming Lally, the pronunciation of the two words of her baptismal name proving to be impossible in their accepted form. Billy had thought it an improvement on what he had always regarded as a fanciful choice of Coral's and he had taken to his daughter's new name with enthusiasm. For a long time Coral alone had remained steadfast in calling Mary Marigold by the name that had been chosen for her but as time passed, defeated by the general acceptance of the diminutive, Coral also took to using Lally for her daughter, Mary Marigold being reserved for moments of disapproval or, more rarely, spontaneous affection.

Coral had few regrets about life as it was lived in Advent Gardens. If Lally was not the robust, intrepid child Coral had envisaged, she was tractable, almost docile, and the most valuable asset in her mother's possession.

Billy was the most accommodating and deluded of husbands and Coral's need to have recourse to indisposition fluctuated as the marriage progressed. By the time Billy had established an alternative source of satisfaction for himself Coral's hypochondria had become part of the fabric of their lives, and Billy neither totally disregarded her complaints nor any longer paid them much attention.

The question of Effie Sweet's return to the senior Bassetts never arose and even when Lally was settled into the kindergarten attached to St Perpetua's there seemed more than ever to occupy Effie as she chortled her way through housework and gardening as she had always done. She appeared to be devoted equally to Coral and Billy, allowing no breeze or ripple of discomfort to engulf Billy, nothing disagreeable nor irksome to overwhelm Coral: Lally she treated as an equal.

In achieving this perfectly tolerable way of life Coral had made only one adjustment unwillingly. The Bassetts of Reskadinnick were old Catholics and before her marriage to Billy, Coral had taken instruction from Canon Washbourne who went once a week to dine with Judith and Terrance Bassett. After tea and before dinner, to which Coral was not invited, Canon Washbourne would instruct her in some aspect of the faith to which she was preparing to surrender herself. Coral had accepted her apostasy from the Wesleyan chapel of her childhood as a small price to pay for social advancement but it was only when Effie Sweet had come to live in Advent Gardens that Coral felt the whole weight of religious obedience descend upon her.

If Judith Bassett had hoped to plant an informer in her son's house she had been unsuccessful, for by insinuating into their lives someone of such unconditional loyalty and lack of discernment all that had been achieved was that Coral now had an ally. An ally, moreover, who seemed unfazed that Coral's practice of her adopted religion had so often been supplanted by her need for rest, aspirin and arrowroot biscuits.

To the astonishment of everyone who knew them, there developed between Coral and Effie Sweet an obligation of dependency which confused those excluded from its closeness and which, it has to be said, some found distasteful. It pleased Effie to be spoken to roughly; she offered it up for her current good cause, resorting to the benefit of her own soul only when nothing more deserving presented itself. This happened rarely as there was nearly always something in the Bassett household in need of a spiritual panacea and Effie cackled and sang her way through the days, happily conscious of improving the chances that Coral or Billy had of receiving a few days remission from their term in purgatory.

Effie accepted without question whatever Coral said and she believed everything that Coral told her. Coral's estimation of her own probity and intelligence was only slightly higher than the opinion Effie Sweet held of her, and neither spite nor uncharitable words, callous or thoughtless acts seemed to affect Effie's cheerful devotion for long. This devotion poured from Effie: it surged and flooded over Coral, swamping her and leaving her stranded and exhausted until she would again call to Effie to come and rescue her, her manner both exasperated and offensive.

When Coral found Effie's proximity too much to bear she would insist that she had a day off; a weekend, or, very occasionally, a whole week in Wenlock Edge, an area to which Effie was unaccountably drawn. Coral had once, very daring, returned Effie to Judith Bassett for three weeks while Billy took his family to Switzerland. Effie always returned after even the shortest of absences with a present for each member of the family and Coral would accept with cold indifference the bottle of Devon Violets or a rosary of improbably pink beads.

Once Effie, chuckling with happy anticipation, had given Lally a red plastic pencil case which opened into three sections. One side was full of mathematical instruments; a protractor and a set square, a compass and a ruler. The other two compartments embraced crayons and pencils, a fountain pen – the first that Lally would ever have owned – a rubber and a pencil sharpener. Lally was mute with delight but almost as soon as she found her voice, Coral's fat little hand snatched the present from the child and she turned to Effie with an expression on her face that stayed in Lally's memory for years.

'I'll take that.' The pencil case was slammed shut.

'Plastic rubbish; I've told you we don't want plastic in this house, Effie. Did you forget or did you deliberately buy this to annoy me? In any case, Lally can't have it, it's much too expensive.' Coral opened her handbag and took out a pound note which she tried to force into Effie's hand. 'I do wish you wouldn't spend your money on us; it only means I'll have to give you some more so it's just as if I've bought the things myself and I certainly wouldn't spend good money on such nonsense.'

'You shouldn't have taken Lally's present away from her.' Effie had let the pound note slip to the floor and now she bent down to pick it up. 'I'll put this in the Missions Box then, I don't want it.' Effie walked towards the door into the hall where the collection box from church stood on a table. There was no burble of laughter, no song, and Effie was humming so quietly that for the first time Coral wondered if she had gone too far. Lally was watching her mother, her face paler than usual but void of emotion: impassive, until you looked at her eyes.

Coral picked up her handbag and spoke to Lally. 'For goodness sake, Mary Marigold, it's only a pencil case and a very nasty one at that. I'll put it away until Christmas; it'll do very well for you to give to Dorcas as I don't suppose she's got a proper pencil case at all.'

'Yes she has.'

'Don't answer me back, and I don't want to hear another word about it. I'm going to lie down for a while as all this has given me a headache. If you're going to play, play quietly and tell Effie to bring me a cup of tea at four.' Coral left the room and Lally took several biscuits from the barrel before going into the garden to sit in the Wendy house and pretend that she was an orphan like Effie or even half an orphan like Dorcas, whose father was dead and whose mother let her do anything.

Lally wasn't often allowed to go to Dorcas's house but Dorcas came to the house in Advent Gardens several times a week straight from school, to have tea with Lally or to play Halma or Old Maid in the kitchen with Effie. Lally couldn't understand why Dorcas never seemed to be afraid of Coral, when she herself spent most of her life frightened of provoking illness or anger in her mother which would rebound on all of them. If Lally understood anything it was that she was so sinful that she was afraid of going to hell before Effie had banked enough indulgences for her sentence to be commuted to years in purgatory.

Lally lay on the old nursery rug which was spread as a carpet on the splintery floor of the Wendy house. Her head rested on Baby Bunting with her feet on Little Miss Muffet and in between the two, magical characters supported the thin little body. Shirley Temple, dimpled, ringleted and bound in black passe-partout, smiled unseeingly down on Lally as she sobbed for the loss and unfairness of a present which had been snatched away out of pique and which she had so longed to possess.

Lally could have hated her mother and wished her dead if Mother Immaculata's cold, calculated words hadn't sifted softly into her mind like the musky dust that had colonised the inside of the Wendy house. They had just learned the fourth commandment and Lally was word perfect — *all contempt, stubbornness, and disobedience to our parents and lawful superiors is forbidden.* Lally lay on the hard, unforgiving floor of the shed and tried to clear her mind by repeating softly to herself, over and over again, '*Of course I love my mother: I do, I do love her. Please, Our Lady, Mother of Mercy, look after her and don't let her be ill because I do love her. I do, I really do,*' until she fell asleep surrounded by Cockle Shells and Silver Bells and a threadbare Little Boy Blue, whose buckled shoes were nearly worn away.

CHAPTER TWO

Coral sat rather upright in bed, which helped to disguise the rolls of flesh which had gathered around her waist and chin, a consequence of her inactive lifestyle. Once she had been plump and fresh, inviting, in the way of a peach before the skin starts to wrinkle over tissue that is on the point of decay. She wore a satin nightdress topped by a short, lace-edged cape, both in eau-de-Nil, which colour, she had been persuaded, would bring out the highlights in her hair.

At this time of the morning Coral had not yet decided how well she was feeling. She would make up her mind after her bath, whether she would dress for a morning's shopping and coffee with one of her friends, or whether it would be a day to stay in a housecoat and to lie on the day bed, blinds lowered to keep out the light, Effie forbidden to bother her unless Coral rang the bell, a brass-crinolined figurine which was left close to hand.

Lally had been in to kiss her mother goodbye and Coral had pulled stray, pale hair from under the confines of St Perpetua's purple beret. 'I do wish you wouldn't hide your hair all the time; it's such a contrast with the mauve that you should make the most of it.' Coral looked at her daughter's water-coloured eyes. 'We can do something about your eyelashes later on when you're older if you don't like them being so pale although I think they make you look very stylish, very striking. I'm afraid you're stuck with your hair but you should try to do the best you can with it.' Coral had teased a frizz of curls around the edge of the beret and Lally had known that once more she would have to face Mother Immaculata's accusation of vanity, too afraid to explain Coral's intervention.

As they walked up the hill to St Perpetua's, Effie noticed the child's distraction but thought that Lally was memorising the morning's catechism. Only Lally knew that she was trying to imagine the difference that thick, dark eyelashes like Dorcas's would make to her life and that the questions she was answering silently in her mind were nothing to do with that morning's catechism, which she knew by heart, but were concerned with the death of her mother, the threat of which could only be held at bay by Lally herself if she assured the voice in her head that she did truly and forever love Coral.

When Effie returned to the house in Advent Gardens she went straight upstairs to collect Coral's breakfast tray, taking with her the morning post. While Coral opened the letters addressed both to her and to Billy, Effie brushed the heavy, copper hair which Coral wore in a tight plait at night. Every morning Effie loosened the confined mane, separating and smoothing it free from tangles, her broad, blunt fingers gently teasing a comb through any snarls until it was restored to its customary order. If Coral was now almost unbecomingly fat, her hair had lost none of its beauty. It was still as thick and as glossy as it had always been and never seemed greasy or too dry, possessing just the right amount of wave to allow Coral to style it in any way she chose.

Now, while Effie sang and giggled and fashioned a French pleat for her, Coral looked in the silver-backed hand mirror that matched the set on her dressing-table and smiled; a secretive, gratified expression which no-one saw but Effie, and Effie had never counted.

'That'll do, Effie. Take the tray away and then come back because we need to make arrangements for Lally's birthday party.' Coral tied a chiffon scarf carefully around her hair, before accepting from Effie a notepad and pencil. 'Pink and white iced buns; an orange jelly and individual ones — strawberry perhaps? Jam tarts and a chocolate bunny blancmange. That'll do, with egg and sardine spread sandwiches and sausage rolls.'

'The cake. Don't forget the cake.' Effie's eyes were excited. This would be the eleventh year that she had made a birthday cake for Lally and each one was a triumph, in spite of wartime shortages. 'I thought this one could have pale yellow icing and daisies in white

27

and green with a darker yellow centre and then the little rabbit candle holders would make it look like spring. White candles, or yellow, what do you think?'

Coral was gathering together envelopes and circulars which were scattered on the humps of her eiderdown and without looking at Effie she said, 'You needn't bother this year, Effie, I've ordered a cake for Mary Marigold: I thought it safer to have one professionally made as I've invited some of the girls who'll be in the senior school with her next year and I can't risk another disaster like we had last time.' Coral handed the bundle of papers to Effie, whose song had died with Coral's words. 'Oh, what's the matter now? It's only a cake, for goodness sake, you'll have plenty of other things to do and it's time Lally had something more grown up than rabbits and daisies.'

Effie thought of the last birthday cake she had made: of how sugar roses had spilled out of tiny baskets, sprays of leaves twining around the handles. She had meant to sprinkle hundreds-and-thousands lightly to enhance the colour of the flowers but too late to stop her, Effie had seen Lally scattering handfuls of the tiny sweets over the top of the finished cake. There was nothing to be done as Effie would never betray the child and although Coral had been furious Billy said that it was certainly the best cake that Effie had yet made and Lally thought it by far the prettiest.

Coral had almost decided to telephone Alma Westley to say that she would be free for lunch but the sight of Effie's eyes, huge and hurt and glittering behind her thick lenses, decided her against it. She would post Dorcas's invitation along with the ones that Lally couldn't distribute at school and meet Alma another day.

Alma Westley was the only friend from the days in Gwavas Terrace that Coral still saw with any regularity, a curious, symbiotic alliance which had proved to be of advantage to both women. There had been a time, when they were much younger and Coral at the very beginning of her life of circumspection and determination, when she had allowed Alma to escape into an existence which Coral envied but into which she was too cautious to follow. Once she was married to Billy Bassett and living in Advent Gardens there was really no necessity for Coral to see Alma again except in the most casual of circumstances and sometimes Coral wondered why she had sought out someone she should have discarded along with all the others, what impenetrable need kept them together when everything about their lives was so dissimilar.

Was it that Coral understood that Alma was the one person she could not mislead; that she needed some core of truth where the artifice and duplicity which made her life one of permanent subterfuge was, just for a little while, unnecessary? Effie Sweet saw Coral only as she was but Alma Westley knew Coral for what she had always been.

Alma had been newly married to Roy Westley and pregnant with her first child when she had run across Coral in the doctor's waiting room and had been surprised at the warmth of Coral's greeting. She had been more surprised yet to find Coral still waiting for her when she came out of the surgery with a prescription for iron tablets and the doctor's advice to take things more easily.

They had gone for a coffee together before Alma had hurried back to work and Coral to buy herself a new navy blue-and-white crêpe smock to wear when she and Billy dined with his parents that evening. Alma and Coral had parted with a promise to keep in touch, which Alma had no intention of honouring and which Coral had every intention of pursuing.

It was as if Coral needed to be near Alma, as if her perceived lack of concern and pragmatic acceptance of her unplanned pregnancy reassured Coral, allowing her to believe that this, her third child, would survive and flourish, bringing with it all that was necessary to fulfil Coral's expectations. It would be the bond between her and Billy that would become indissoluble as soon as their child was born.

Coral began to telephone Alma in the evenings and to drive to the little house in Dobells Path after Mass on Sunday mornings while Billy met his friends at the golf club and Effie prepared lunch. Coral was surprised but undeterred when Alma would appear downstairs to answer the insistent peal of the bell wearing a dressing-gown, with her hair dishevelled, sometimes even with traces of the previous day's make-up still on her face.

Alma would put the kettle on the old gas stove and make tea, listening inattentively to Coral's news. They seldom talked of their marriages, but of the days spent growing up in the little, similar houses up by the Rec. Coral's parents were dead and the house occupied by other tenants but Alma's mother stayed on alone in the downstairs room of the house in Gwavas Terrace which had become her encompassing space where she slept and ate and watched the legs of people passing above her on the pavement.

Alma did her mother's washing and paid her bills and, as Roy had no car, she struggled on the bus with her mother's groceries which she bought when she shopped for her own in the new supermarket which was so much cheaper than the little shop on the corner. Coral knew all this but never offered to help and Alma never thought to ask.

Their daughters had been born three weeks apart; Mary Marigold Bassett in an expensive room with a view in a private nursing home overlooking Mounts Bay and Dorcas Westley in the maternity ward of Penalverne Hospital. Coral took Mary Marigold to an afternoon clinic quite conscientiously but they sat apart, isolated, as if afraid that either of them might be contaminated by other children. Coral removed communal toys from the child, wiping, cleaning, keeping themselves at a distance from everyone except Alma and Dorcas.

Alma had worked until two weeks before Dorcas's birth and knew that the time she had exclusively with her daughter was limited, circumscribed by Roy Westley's capacity to remain employed. When Dorcas was old enough to be left with Roy for a few hours Alma took a job in a bookie's on a Saturday afternoon, which she laughed away to Roy saying that now both of them were indebted to the Turf.

Occasionally Dorcas was asked to tea at the house in Advent Gardens and once or twice Coral had tried to give Alma parcels of clothes that Lally was supposed to have outgrown. They were the only times that Coral ever saw Alma angry and there had been a coolness between them for a while, not entirely resolved until Roy Westley's early death from a heart attack on a zebra crossing on a day of rare good fortune and drizzling rain.

Coral, detached and protected in her pleasant house, indulged by Effie Sweet, and immune from imagination, was astonished to find that Alma mourned her husband with the kind of visible grief that Coral found disconcerting. To Coral, Roy Westley had been no more than a peripheral figure on the margin of Alma's life; someone whom Coral seldom saw and in whom she had very little interest. Now, with his absence assuming the importance that his presence had never enjoyed, Coral found herself excluded by Alma's distress from the one friend on whom she had always counted.

Over the coffee cups and among the rum babas and chocolate éclairs at The Buttery, Coral was swift to agree with her acquaintances that *yes, it was a shock; so young and full of life and that poor little girl — what was her name again?*

Dorcas, that's right, Dorcas, what will happen to her? The same age as Lally isn't she, and surely Coral had known Alma Westley when they were girls — hadn't they been neighbours at one time?

Many scores were settled over the cream cakes and light lunches in the cafés of Penalverne but Coral, practised in dissimulation, wary and unforgiving, spoke only of how she thought she might help Dorcas, mainly for Lally's sake as the two girls seemed to have struck up a friendship how, Coral wasn't quite sure, as they moved in such different circles. She convinced no-one but fear of what might follow a challenge to this statement kept everyone silent, at least until Coral went to powder her nose.

Leaning over a basin to see herself in speckled, resistant glass or admiring herself in flattering pink mirrors Coral applied pale powder as thickly as if she were battering fish: its distinctive, cloying smell always seemed to surround her and gave her a face which wore the mask of a middle-aged clown. Coral had a very short neck and over the years her head seemed to have to struggle to raise the heavy coils of hair above her shoulders, which had become too broad and too heavy and which she tried to disguise with expensive clothes. She was only partly successful and was unable to see, as everyone else did, the resemblance she now bore to a small, square box.

Coral's lack of imagination precluded her from understanding the depth of the hurt she had caused Effie

33

over Lally's birthday cake and she noticed only that Effie was unusually silent, the humming and snatches of song which were her audible *doppelgänger*, silenced. The atmosphere remained subdued, at lunch time Effie bringing home-made soup and an egg custard to Coral lying on the day bed in the bay window of the room at the front of the house. Coral had decided after all that she was feeling debilitated, a frailty which could only be assuaged by constant attention from someone, and Effie was the only person available.

Effie's withdrawal into hurt feelings was rare and perceived by Coral to be sulking and Coral knew only one way to provoke a reaction from her in this mood. She bullied Effie: continuously and viciously, until Effie capitulated and started to cry. Then Coral would assure Effie of her continued affection for her; her appreciation of all that Effie did and the absurdity of Effie's reaction to Coral's playful words. This reconciliation was always ratified by the presentation of a gift, and Effie would accept the beads that needed restringing or the powder compact which had only a small amount of its enamel missing, with humble astonishment.

There was an empty three-pound chocolate box on Effie's chest of drawers – itself a gift from Coral when she had eaten all the chocolates which it had contained – and in this faintly scented, cardboard-sided casket Effie kept all her treasures. There was a ring which Effie thought to be a ruby and around which she had wound grey darning wool to keep it from slipping off her finger; a tiny pencil which had on its end what looked to Effie like a tiny, silver top hat and which had once been paired with a diary; a few small shells which Lally had picked up on the beach and every card and drawing which the child had ever given her.

Effie was always astonished at the riches in her possession and occasionally she allowed Lally to play with them, explaining in detail the provenance of each curiosity, chuckling with shared pleasure as Lally carefully replaced each tarnished piece in its accustomed place.

It was Effie, knowing how Lally loved the contained disposition of the objects in the chocolate box, who suggested to Coral that the little girl might enjoy having a doll's house for her birthday. Instead of the usual brusque rejection of her idea, Coral had seized on it with enthusiasm and Billy had ordered the de luxe version to be delivered in good time to be displayed as the main attraction at Lally's party. The house which arrived was triple fronted with a red-tiled roof. Painted wistaria grew up the walls and around the green tinplate windows and there was a concealed battery which lit torch bulbs in the tiny lights which hung in every room.

Coral had told Alma about the doll's house and Alma remembered that somewhere she had a box of furniture that had been given to her by the old lady who ran the Sunday school at the chapel where she and Coral had gone together as children. Alma had eventually found the box under the bed, pushed in with all those things she intended to sort out one day.

The carton had once held a pair of her father's working boots and still smelled faintly of leather. The lid was rough with dust, and stiff, but Alma eased it off and unwrapped each little parcel with care, marvelling at the delicacy of the silver filigree of which the sofa and chairs were made, reluctant to part with the tiny pewter candlesticks and the rocking cradle or the copper moulds and earthenware bowls meant for the kitchen.

Dorcas had been standing watching her mother unwrap these hidden treasures. 'You're not really going to give those to Lally are you?'

'What do you suggest we give her then? We can't afford anything very nice and these would do, wouldn't they?'

'*I'd* like them.'

'Well, it does seem a pity not to hang on to them. I remember Miss Couch saying that they were very old, American some of them, and I suppose they might be worth a bit. How about if we give Lally one or two things? Say, the rocking horse and the baby bath?'

'Not the rocking horse,' Dorcas spoke firmly. 'She can have the bath and the clothes airer and the hot-water can. Nothing else.'

Alma looked at her daughter. 'Why this sudden ungenerosity? I thought you got on with Lally now.'

'I like her a bit.'

'But?'

'But, I *hate* Aunt Coral. She's fat and smelly and she tells lies.'

'Dorcas!'

'Well, it's true. I wish I didn't have to go there so much. Uncle Billy always smells of beer when he kisses me and Effie sings about funny things all the time and Lally's afraid of doing anything in case it's a sin and makes Aunt Coral ill.' Dorcas leaned on the table and looked at her mother. 'Do you think it's a sin to give me bacon rinds to eat?'

'What on earth do you mean by that?'

'Last week when I was there we had bacon and eggs for tea – well, Lally had bacon and eggs and I had one egg and her bacon rinds. Effie tried to give me some bacon too but Aunt Coral put it all on Lally's plate and I heard her saying that the rinds were good enough for me.'

'Look at me, Dorcas.' Alma took her daughter's arm, shaking it lightly. 'Is this true?'

'Of course it's true. It's sinful to tell lies, Lally told me. She said we'd go to hell if we told lies and I don't want to go to hell. You roast in the fires for ever and ever and the devil pokes you with a big toasting fork.'

'That's nonsense, Dorcas. You don't have to believe everything that Lally tells you, you know.' Alma looked at the inch-long zinc bath in her hand. 'Perhaps we should keep all these things together and I'll find something else, a book, for you to give to Lally. Dorcas.'

'Yes.'

'You are absolutely *sure* about the bacon rinds aren't you?'

The child nodded, pretending to pour water from

the tiny metal can into the bath which her mother held. 'Lally says that if I make a fuss or if I don't do what I'm told Aunt Coral will be ill, and if she dies it'll be my fault that Lally's an orphan. She says she'll probably have to enter the convent and become a saint like the Little Flower. What's the Little Flower, Alma?'

'No idea, and Lally won't be an orphan, she'll still have her father.'

'Lally says . . .'

'Stop it, Dorcas, I don't want to hear another word about what Lally says.' Alma collected the scattered bits of furniture together with one angry sweep of her hand, dropping them into the box and jamming on the lid. 'I'll speak to Coral about your food.'

'She won't like it.'

'Well, do you like eating liver sandwiches and bacon rinds?'

Dorcas shook her head, stroking the table with the end of her pigtail. 'She might not like it so much that she might even die.'

'Listen to me, my bird. Coral Bassett is as strong as an ox and she always was as mean as ditchwater and I wouldn't send you there if there was anywhere else you could go.' Alma looked sideways at her daughter, wondering how much she should say. 'Anyway, it won't be for much longer so please just put up with it for a little while like a good girl. And, Dorcas, don't tell *anyone* what I've just said. Promise?'

'Promise.'

Alma knew that Dorcas would keep her word and she pulled the child into her arms. 'How about asking Mr Jelbart if he's got a broccoli crate we could have and we'll make a doll's house of our own? We've got all this lovely furniture and I believe there's even a family of dolls in there somewhere. *And* I think we should have fish and chips for tea so go and put your coat on while I find my purse.' Too soon, Alma thought, to tell Dorcas about Vernon Orme; too big a secret to entrust to a child, even one as reliable as her daughter.

It had been raining and the air was clammy, the day too warm for spring. Dorcas struggled into her school mackintosh, the sleeves too short, the belt secured on the last eyelet around her sturdy body. 'You need a new coat.' Alma looked at her daughter with appraising eyes. 'We'll go and get one on Saturday; I was going to get you a dress for the party but you really do need a coat. I hadn't noticed how much you'd grown.'

Dorcas pulled up the check-lined hood and tied the cords under her chin. She looked plain and resolute and Alma longed to make up to her all that she missed. 'I can wear my summer dress but ...' Dorcas hesitated, '... do you think ... could we possibly ... afford some shoes? All the others have party shoes and I'll have to wear my slippers because Aunt Coral doesn't let me wear my outdoor shoes in the house. She says you don't know what I might have stepped in walking over there because the streets around the Council School aren't cleaned very well.'

Alma, remembering the days when she and Coral had walked those same streets together, jumping puddles wearing leaky shoes which their fathers mended; dodging piles of dung that someone would collect with a shovel and the coal bucket to use as fertiliser, forced a smile before she looked at Dorcas. 'Shoes it is. Patent leather or silver, what would Modom prefer?'

'Red,' Dorcas said, 'red shiny shoes.'

CHAPTER THREE

'*The Little White Horse*, how nice, but too old for Lally just yet. You may spend all your time reading, Dorcas, but Mary Marigold has so many other interests and activities.'

Dorcas looked at Coral; saw the dissembling smile, the tiny cracks where sweat was beginning to undermine the patina on her face and she wanted to snatch the book back from those podgy fingers: she wanted to go and sit in a corner and read it herself, uninterrupted by calls for circles to be formed or partners to be chosen. No-one ever chose Dorcas and she often found herself paired with Effie or Uncle Billy, whose sympathetic eyes she ignored, repelled by the smell of peppermint which came from him in gusts as he became breathless with dancing or dashing for the last chair in the middle of the floor.

Dorcas watched Coral read the fly leaf and then put

the present she had brought for Lally at the back of the pile on the table under the window. Before Alma had wrapped the book she had made Dorcas write inside it: *To Lally, on her birthday. Love from Dorcas.* 'Coral won't like that,' she said, 'but at least it'll stop her from passing it on to someone else. Put your finger on the knot for me, lovey.' Alma had tied thin red string around the parcel wrapped in paper which had been saved from last year, ironed and trimmed so that it looked almost new. 'I'll leave it with your dress and shoes at Lally's so you can change there after school and I'll come and pick you up at seven.'

'We're going to be allowed to see the doll's house after tea. Only Lally's allowed to touch it Aunt Coral says, but we can all have a look at it.'

'That will be nice for you.' Dorcas glanced sideways at her mother but Alma's face was guileless. 'Mrs Matthews said that Heidi's been invited to the party and you quite like her, don't you? She's not one of the St Perpetua's crowd either so try and stick with her.' Dorcas nodded, toe inching into the worn part of the carpet until she had stretched the already loose threads into a hole. She knew that she would be the only one there in a summer frock but the thought of her red shoes, shiny, silver-buckled and new, made up for that.

The girls from St Perpetua's arrived together at the house in Advent Gardens and Dorcas could hear music and see yellow light coming from the big room at the front of the house when she stood alone in the hall. She had pushed the bell but no-one had come to see who was there so she had opened the door and let herself in. Dorcas waited but still no-one came to greet her and, after a while, she went into the small conservatory which served as a cloakroom, to hang up her mackintosh and to discard her shoes before walking up the stairs to Lally's bedroom.

The landing was almost circular, doors positioned at exact intervals around the wall. Two-thirds of the way along the right-hand side there was a break where a passage led to a smaller staircase and the room where Effie slept. To balance this inconsistency there was, on the left-hand side, an alcove where Coral had placed a scroll-ended sofa covered in gold brocade. Anyone sitting here could remain concealed but with a view over a balcony of all the doors on the ground floor, a bull's eye glass enabling the watcher to see whoever came and went at the front door.

Dorcas's dress was hanging on the back of the door in Lally's bedroom and she changed quickly, tossing her tunic and blouse onto the pile of mauve tweed coats lying on the bed, each with a beret placed neatly beside it. Dorcas did up the six daisy-shaped buttons down the front of her dress and then looked for her shoes. They weren't under the bed, nor in the cupboard where Lally's clothes were hanging, colourless, their style curiously outdated. Dorcas crawled around the floor on her hands and knees, moving the rugs, the stool, the wastepaper basket under Lally's desk. She rummaged through the pile of thick mauve coats, scattering berets like a burrowing animal as sickness and panic squeezed her chest and made her face burn with apprehension. Without her new shoes she wouldn't walk into that room full of girls who knew each other, nor stand in her slippers in the doorway and watch Aunt Coral's hand reach out for her, gold charms on her bracelet chinking softly together, salmon-pink nails like little claws waiting to draw her into the game.

Dorcas slipped out of Lally's bedroom and went across the landing, the thick cream carpet soft under her feet. In the alcove she sat on the edge of the over-stuffed gold brocade seat, the material cold and slippery against the back of her legs. As Dorcas sat there she saw a movement below her and to the right and Effie Sweet came out of the door which led to the back of the house. In her hands were Dorcas's red shoes and Effie carried them to the conservatory beside the front door, shuffling across the black and white tiles of the hall. She came out, shutting the door behind her, and Dorcas could see the bony shoulders heaving with suppressed glee as Effie walked silently across the floor, disappearing out of sight again like a wraith.

Dorcas waited, afraid that Effie might be watching in the shadows: she often did, when only a burst of laughter or the persistent hum of a suppressed song betrayed her. Silently Dorcas slid down the stairs staying close to the wall and with one more glance to her right, she opened the door to the cloakroom as quietly as possible and went inside. Her new shoes stood next to her outdoor brogues, which had been placed neatly together, the laces dropped inside their open throat. Dorcas washed her face, running damp hands over the front of her hair, watching the shiny newness out of the corner of her eye in case it disappeared again. Finally she allowed herself the pleasure of putting one foot, and then the other, into her red shoes; doing up the silver buckle, the strap still stiff from lack of use. She pulled up her socks and went towards the sound of the party.

It was Billy who saw Dorcas and put an arm around her saying, 'Make way for a little one,' helping her to find a place in the circle on the floor. Pass-the-Parcel had already started, Coral strumming on the piano, sitting in a position which meant she was just able to see where the package was in transit. She allowed Dorcas a turn at pulling off brown paper and string before manipulating the music to allow a winner to emerge. Coral's whim fell on the niece of Penalverne's Mayor Elect, who thanked her hostess very prettily before putting her prize on the table next to Lally's presents. In the centre of all those layers of paper, each tied with an easily ripped apart knot, had been a brown leather manicure set which Dorcas knew to be the one which Effie had brought home from a holiday in Sidmouth as an offering to Coral.

Dorcas looked around the circle, seeking Heidi Matthews but she saw only the girls whose mauve tweed coats lay on the bed upstairs: St Perpetua's girls whose fathers owned cars and whose mothers didn't need to go out to work and who met each other for coffee and shopping expeditions to Truro where they bought their shoes at a shop in Quay Street, a pair to match each outfit.

'A quiet game before tea,' Coral said, 'and then, afterwards, we'll bring out the doll's house and Lally can put all her new furniture in place.' Coral's smile seemed to include everyone but she looked directly at Dorcas as she said, 'So many of you bought such thoughtful gifts for my girl's wee house.' Dorcas met her gaze unwaveringly and it was Coral who looked away.

Coral was wearing a dress of Prince of Wales check which seen from a distance looked grey, the tiny black-and-white pattern emerging as you got closer, the red stripe which ran crossways through the cloth revealing itself only at very close quarters. The dress was too tight and as Coral leaned over Dorcas with a plate of fish paste sandwiches, Dorcas could see dark half-moons of sweat outlining each armpit and she could smell Coral's face powder and something sour and stale which seemed to enclose her. Alma always smelled clean and sharp like lily-of-the-valley or lemons and suddenly Dorcas was engulfed by longing for her mother: for her to wink at Dorcas as if they alone shared a secret worth knowing; for her arms to warm Dorcas, to keep her safe from patronage and pretence.

Dorcas looked at the plate of sandwiches that Coral

was holding out to her and said, 'I'd rather have a cake, please.'

'Come along, Dorcas, don't be difficult: you know the rules, bread first, then cake,' Coral was smiling the same half-smile that concealed from nearly everyone her real intentions. Dorcas saw again Effie Sweet walking across the hall, red shoes in hand, Effie who did nothing without Coral's imprimatur, and she knew with a child's absolute conviction that Coral had hidden the shoes and that she, Dorcas, would never forgive her.

Dorcas ignored the plate held out to her, conscious that several of Lally's friends had heard her humiliated by the reprimand and that they were watching her. She stretched out a hand to one of the silver-doilyed plates of buns flanking the birthday cake in the middle of the table and chose one with pink icing decorated by a flower made from half a cherry and leaves of angelica. Lally was looking at Dorcas, staring at her, as she ate the half-cherry, the angelica leaves, and then started to lick the soft pink icing before tearing off the crinkled wax-paper case and eating the rest of the cake. Dorcas wiped her fingers on an embroidered napkin and smiled directly at Lally and Lally quickly looked away, aware that Coral would be bound to notice if she appeared to be supporting Dorcas. Lally's egg sandwich seemed suddenly loathsome, an evil smell translated into taste and she left it on her plate while she twisted her fingers together in her lap, hating Dorcas for challenging Coral's authority.

'Don't you like your nice sandwich?' Effie's voice was soft in Lally's ear and Lally shook her head, knowing speech would bring tears. Effie wrapped a napkin around the little triangular sandwich and palmed it so swiftly that it might never have been. 'Have a sausage roll instead; I made them tiny specially – just the way you like them.' Lally was about to refuse when Effie went on, 'Better to, my lover, we don't want any fuss later on, do we?' Effie put a roll in front of Lally and moved away, sibilant hisses which might have been song, trailing behind her.

The cake, the professionally made birthday cake, was the centrepiece of the tea party and now Coral cleared a space in front of Lally, and Billy moved the stand so that Lally could blow out the eleven candles and then make the first incision with the special knife which had been used to cut all the previous cakes that Effie had made for her. The blade and the handle were both silver plated and the knife looked like a dagger, huge in Lally's small hands.

'Make a wish, Lally, but don't tell or it won't come true.' Effie was excited, more excited than any of the guests around the table and she laughed and snuffled, light from the burning candles reflected in the thick convex lenses of her glasses. Lally blew out the flames and then screwed up her eyes. Her face was partly hidden from Coral, who stood behind her daughter's chair, and it was Dorcas who was transfixed by the expression on Lally's face. The child had closed her eyes and her face, always pale, seemed almost transparent, a pattern of blue veins clearly visible under the skin of her cheeks and down into her neck. Dorcas felt that if she tried hard enough she could see right through Lally's translucent eyelids and travel down those blue-veined highways straight into her heart. She forced herself to look away, to concentrate on Lally's hands, both of them clasped around the heavy-bladed knife.

Lally seemed to take a long time to make her wish; she stood very still, time suspended, until at last she opened her eyes, took a deep breath, and some colour washed back into her face, occluding the blue of her veins. 'I've made my wish,' she said, and then raised the knife and slammed it down into the middle of the cake with all her strength. Dorcas shivered but no-one else seemed to have noticed anything unusual as Lally quietly handed the knife to Effie who cut enough slices to go around.

After tea, while Coral and Billy went to collect the doll's house, Lally's guests slid and giggled their way to the cloakroom, ostensibly to wash their hands. Dorcas watched them grouping and whispering, wondering why Lally seemed to have chosen to align herself with them. She was treating Dorcas in the offhand manner she usually reserved for Effie, isolating her as alien, a perceived interloper in the circle of which Lally was becoming an element.

In a misguided attempt to save money Coral always kept the house at just under a comfortable temperature and Dorcas was chilly in her thin dress. The alternative would be to fetch her grey school cardigan but she would rather have frozen altogether than to have shown such weakness.

'Here, borrow this; I had to wear my winter dress as it's the only thing I had that was clean enough and I'm much too hot.' Dorcas looked at the girl who had spoken to her, ready to refuse. 'Go on, I don't need it and you look frozen. You're Dorcas aren't you? I'm Gerry Jarvie. We've only just moved here so I don't know many people but I think Mrs Bassett sees me as a suitable friend for Lally. Isn't this party too *awful?*'

Dorcas took the blue, hand-knitted cardigan which the older girl handed to her. 'Thanks.' She stopped, afraid to say any more, then took a chance and said in a rush, 'Yes, it is. Lally's parties are always awful and I only come because my mother makes me. She's known Aunt Coral — Mrs Bassett — for ever.'

'Come on then, we'll brave it together. Did you bring something for the "wee house", as your Aunt Coral put it? Sounds like a lav although I'm sure that Mrs B would never be so vulgar.'

'No, a book; and it's too old for Lally Aunt Coral says, but that's probably because Mummy made me write in it so that Aunt Coral can't pass it on to someone else — she does that all the time.' Gerry pulled a face that made Dorcas laugh and they walked together towards the front room.

A table had been moved into the centre of the floor and on it stood Lally's doll's house. Grouped around it were the small pieces of donated furniture that Lally was to put in their appointed places as if she were participating in some arcane ritual. Coral sat beside Lally on the sofa, legs crossed at the ankle and hands folded, thumbs upright and pressed together. As Lally picked up a green-painted bed or a moquette-covered armchair Coral would murmur something to her and Lally would place the piece of furniture in position. There seemed to be no disagreement, no protestation if Coral gently guided Lally's hand away from her chosen site to another which Coral preferred. Gradually the house was filled, its four rooms furnished exactly as Coral wished them to be.

Lally kept her doll's house for the rest of her life and not once, not by the slightest margin, did she change the position of a spoon or a vase. Sometimes, over the years, she and Dorcas were allowed to play with the house but not as children play, on the floor, the toy a focus of imagination and occasional mishap. It was, without exception, placed on a table and always, before the game ended, each chair, each cupboard, each rug and lamp was restored to the place appointed for it by Coral, long ago on Lally's eleventh birthday.

Now the green tin door was closed and Lally turned the miniature tin handle to keep her property secure. Dorcas was bored and put out a hand to unlatch a mullioned window but Coral's hand grasped hers before she had a chance to complete the manoeuvre. 'I'm sure you'd like to have something like this, Dorcas, but it's very, very special and only for my special little girl.' Coral put an arm around Lally, kissing her on the cheek while her gaze stayed firmly on Dorcas.

'Actually,' Dorcas said, 'actually, Aunt Coral, my doll's house is just as nice as this one.' Dorcas could feel her heart beating so hard that she thought it would show through her skin, her summer dress, her borrowed cardigan.

'Now, Dorcas, you don't have to make things up. We understand, but that was an unkind thing to say and I think you should apologise to Lally.'

Dorcas turned to Lally who was wearing a dress of pale green taffeta with sleeves so puffed that they made the fragile, childish arms which emerged from them look emaciated. A deeper green bow made some attempt to tame Lally's hair and on her feet were black glacé kid shoes with a pompom on the toe, black elastic crossed at her thin ankles. Lally looked at Dorcas and looked away again. Coral's arm was still around her, white blotches from the pressure of her mother's fingers spreading and joining across the listless, defenceless arms.

'I didn't mean to be rude, Lally, but my doll's house *is* nice; it's just different, that's all.' Dorcas turned to Coral, 'Mummy found all the furniture old Miss Couch gave her when she was a little girl. She said you'd remember Miss Couch as she used to give both of you a ha'penny to put in the collection plate each Sunday. We made a house and put everything in it and Mummy says a lot of the things are quite valuable but that they should be played with.'

'That old stuff? I'd have thrown it out long ago but I suppose it's better than nothing.' Coral's face was expressionless, the implacable smile settled in place.

She remembered Miss Couch all right: an elderly, eccentric spinster who had stayed at home to look after her parents and once they had both gone to their just reward she had never seen the necessity of changing anything in the home they had shared. Miss Couch had lived out the rest of her long life almost exactly as her parents had done, accepting only the installation of electricity, and that with reluctance.

Coral remembered the sea horses and the shells with a rainbow trapped inside them; the ostrich egg and the tiny embroidered shoes which looked as if they had been made for a baby but which were meant for a Chinese lady. She remembered the bath with a plunger instead of a plug and its wide mahogany surround and the steps which you had to climb to be tall enough to get into the bath at all. She remembered the blue flowers printed inside the lavatory bowl and the tassels hanging from the edges of the chenille cloth that covered the table in Miss Couch's drawing room.

Alma had been Miss Couch's favourite, of course, allowed to collect hymn books and to give out the weekly stamps to be stuck onto the Sunday school card which was each child's passport to the annual Tea Treat in the summer. Once or twice Coral had been allowed to go with Alma to Miss Couch's house, to sit at the red-clothed table to look through a bioscope at pictures of kings and queens and palms and elephants, all of them stiff and still and all in three dimensions.

If they were good and quiet and didn't scatter crumbs from the small, hard rock cakes they were given to eat, Miss Couch would place the solitaire board between them and watch, smiling to herself, as they failed each time to leave just one of the striped and brilliantly coloured marbles in the centre of the board. Very occasionally Miss Couch would bring out her Sunday books and allow the girls to look at illustrations of Daniel, daringly defying the lion or Jonah, joyful in the jaws of the whale, or a leper or a blind man or a cripple carrying his thin mattress over his shoulder, capering with happiness. Miss Couch believed these books to be the only suitable reading for the sabbath but she had others as well and once Coral had held in her hand a birthday book, each page hand-painted with pansies and maidenhair fern. The pansies each wore the face of a child and the spaces for names were nearly all filled in, the ink faded to a rusty brown. Coral ached to own the silken-paged, purple-covered book but Miss Couch took it back from her hands and suggested that she and Alma might like to play carefully with the mah-jong set before they had to go home.

Coral remembered it all: the ha' pennies taken from a chamois bag, one given to each child who sat at the front of the chapel on the Sunday school benches. Alma and Coral each brought a threepenny bit with them but Miss Couch made no distinction between those who had and those who had not. Oh, Coral remembered Miss Couch very well, with her steel spectacles and large teeth and tiny, tightly contained bun under an old-fashioned straw, stabbed through with two crossed hat pins like swords over a fireplace, and she remembered Miss Couch's face, as grey and set as the local granite on the day she called to see Coral's parents to tell them that their daughter was a thief.

Coral never went to Miss Couch's house again and, frantic with apprehension, threw far into the stream that ran alongside the Rec. the miniature dining-room chair that she had taken and hidden under a handkerchief in the pocket of her school knickers. She watched it sink beneath the waving green weed and disappear into the mud that covered old pram wheels and jam jars and the bones of old Mr Roskilly's dog who had slipped its lead and drowned when Coral was taking it for a walk. If Mrs Paice had any suspicion at all that what Miss Couch had told her was true she chose to remain unconvinced, but Coral was withdrawn at once from the Sunday school and Alma continued to go alone, her collection tied in a handkerchief; too hot in summer, too cold in winter but uncomplaining.

Alma's unconventional friendship with the old lady continued, visits to her house a highlight in the monochrome but contented life she lived with her parents in Gwavas Terrace. It was on Alma's tenth birthday that she was given the doll's house furniture, Miss Couch emphasising that she must take care of it. 'It's antique, Alma. Do you know what that means?'

'Very old, Miss Couch.'

'Indeed. My father brought it from America before I was born and I'm very old, too, you know. I'm giving it to you because I have no family of my own and because I know that you'll take care of it when I'm gone.'

'Where are you going to, Miss Couch? Is it ... is it Torquay?' A visit to Torquay was the current pinnacle of Alma's worldly ambition and she could think of nowhere her friend would enjoy more.

'To a far, far better place, my dear, but for now I want you to promise me that you will always keep my little treasures safe.'

'Oh! I will. And if you come back for a visit from the far, far better place you'll be able to see how well I've looked after them.'

'Alma?'

'Yes, Miss Couch.'

'I have to tell you something regrettable.' Alma was laying the table with plates the size of her little finger nail and she stopped to look at the old lady, afraid she had mistaken her generosity. 'One of the dining-room chairs is missing so I am obliged to give you an incomplete set of three. I'm sorry.'

'Don't be sorry, Miss Couch, there's one for father, one for mother and one for me, just like the three bears, and that's enough.'

'You're a good child, Alma, but you must beware of people who try to take advantage of your trusting nature.'

'I'll be careful, really I will, but I wish you weren't going away. I like visiting you and I like it best now that it's just the two of us.'

Alma's treasures were wrapped up again in tissue paper and Miss Couch replaced them in the basket where they had lain for so long. The basket was round and ribbed and covered in glass beads. There were crystal and ruby and sapphire, and larger, opaque ones like milk, and one or two like the sea at Porthcurno, neither green nor blue but a colour which existed in the inner eye. Alma let her fingers glide along the smooth surface of the beads. 'Did your father bring this from America too?'

'No, he brought that from Africa.' Miss Couch's face was considerate. 'It's very old as well and I thought your mother might like it to put her sewing things in – if she can find a suitable box for the furniture.' Miss Couch put her hands on the arms of her chair and pulled herself to her feet with difficulty. To Alma's surprise she felt cold fingers on her cheek as Miss Couch turned the child's face towards her. 'Remember, little Alma, don't trust everyone. My life might have been very different if someone had told me that years ago.' There were tears in the eyes behind the cruel steel spectacles and Miss Couch bent down to kiss the child's cheek. 'You must go home now, Alma, but think of me sometimes when you play with the furniture.'

Clementine Couch died two weeks later and Alma named the mother doll after her, sitting it on one of the silver chairs in the incomplete set of three.

✳   ✳   ✳

'I'd like to see your doll's house.' Gerry Jarvie spoke to Dorcas just loudly enough for Coral to hear. 'What did you make it out of?'

Dorcas took a deep breath. 'A crate: a broccoli crate we got from Mr Jelbart, and we had a book of wallpaper samples that I use to paint on, so we covered the walls with them.' Dorcas's voice became confident as she saw that Gerry's interest was genuine. 'You can come and see it if you like. I'm making pictures for the walls at the moment and rugs for the floors, but you can help if you want to.'

'I'll come on Saturday, if your mother doesn't mind.'

'I don't expect she will; my mother doesn't mind much and besides,' Dorcas dropped her voice, 'if you come to our house I shan't have to come here and Mummy won't mind that at all.'

The two girls were walking upstairs together, Gerry to put on her coat and Dorcas to collect her discarded school clothes. Dorcas struggled out of the blue cardigan and handed it back to Gerry. 'Thanks for the lend.' She looked at her new friend. 'You don't seem like the other girls from St Perpetua's. Most of them don't want to know me; they just stare and giggle and put on a funny accent when they *do* talk to me.'

'Does it worry you?' Gerry pulled two sweets out of her pocket and gave one to Dorcas. 'Pinched these from the bowl on the sideboard in the dining room.'

'A bit, because Lally's my oldest friend and when she's with them she's just like them. She's sort of OK when we're on our own though.'

'Well, you're the only person I've met since we moved here that I want to be friends with, so whatever plans your Aunt Coral has about making me and Lally into bosom companions, she won't succeed.'

'Oh, but she will, Gerry. Aunt Coral makes people do whatever she wants because if they don't she gets ill and then Lally thinks it's all her fault.'

'Well, I'm sorry about Lally but if I tell my mother that I don't want to be with her all the time, she won't make me. She believes so in freedom of choice that it got her in trouble with our last parish priest ...' Gerry stopped and Coral pushed open the bedroom door, smiling her imposter's smile as she looked at the two girls.

'Well, my goodness, you two *are* good at hiding yourselves away: you're the last ones to be collected and both your mothers are here so hurry up.' Coral looked around Lally's bedroom as if to check that the primrose flounces on the counterpane still hung undefiled to the floor; that the curtains of yellow and white Regency stripe hung unsullied, caught back with a twisted rope of old gold. She straightened the sheepskin rug with her toe and spoke to no-one in particular, looking over Gerry's head at the crucifix which hung over the head of the little white bed. 'I didn't realise that you'd become friends so quickly; Lally *will* be pleased, two of her best friends getting on so well together.' Coral stood aside for Dorcas and Gerry to leave the room ahead of her as if they might even yet take away with them something of value which belonged to Lally, but she put a delaying hand on Gerry's arm. 'I'm going to ask your mother if you'd like to come and play with Lally next Saturday. I thought you two little girls might like a picnic in the Wendy house.'

Gerry smiled at Coral, and Dorcas was captivated to hear the genuine regret with which the other girl managed to colour her voice. 'I'm so sorry, Mrs Bassett, but I've already arranged to go and see Dorcas. We're going to paint pictures and make rugs for her doll's house.' She slipped out of Coral's grasp and followed Dorcas down the stairs, well pleased with the resentment she knew she had left behind her.

Alma and Frances Jarvie were talking together in the hall when the girls clattered across the tiles towards them. 'Mummy, please can I go to Dorcas's house on Saturday? We're going to paint tiny pictures for her doll's house and have fish and chips for lunch.'

'It sounds as if you've got it all arranged. Is it all right with you, Mrs Westley? Do say if it's not.'

Alma looked at Dorcas, at her unsuitable dress and her eager eyes, aware that Coral was listening for her answer as she came slowly down the stairs. 'Dorcas would love to have a friend for the day.' Alma turned towards Coral. 'It'll give you a rest as well, Coral; I expect you need it after today. I hope it's not all been too much for you. Head not troubling you?' Alma's feigned interest in

Coral's well-being was for the benefit of Frances Jarvie and a flicker of amusement passed between them, a conspiracy not lost on Coral who clasped plump hands together across her chest, the smile she managed indicative neither of assent nor disagreement but seeming to contain all the patient endurance of a mother who would sacrifice even her health for her daughter's happiness.

Effie, who was tidying away wrapping paper and wrinkled balloons, and who had done all the work for the party in any case, suddenly began to sing. The erstwhile guests moved down the path together with the sound of, *Thine are the graces unclaimed by another, sinless and beautiful star of the sea*, sounding after them through the open window until silenced, abruptly cut short in mid screech by the sound of falling cutlery, metallic and jagged in the evening air. Alma and Frances Jarvie looked at one another and smiled with complicity, unaware that Effie was whimpering and sobbing, crouched on the carpet, gathering together knives and cake forks and spoons which Coral had knocked out of her hand, Effie herself ricocheting off the edge of the sideboard as she stumbled and fell.

Coral closed the dining-room door on the disturbance and went to play with Lally's new doll's house, impeccable in its immutability, pristine in the constancy of its order.

CHAPTER FOUR

'Does your mother always have to work on Saturdays?'
Gerry Jarvie was sprawled on the sofa looking at herself
in the glass which hung over the fireplace. She moved her
head from side to side watching as her face slid in and
out of focus like an image in a fairground maze. The air
in the small room was heavy, the smell of fish and chips
drifting and settling, their promise of delight dissipated
as soon as the greasy plates had been scraped clean.

'Quite often, but only in the morning and she never
leaves me alone all day. If I'm safe at Aunt Coral's she
sometimes goes out with her boyfriend after work. Dorcas
looked sideways at Gerry. 'She doesn't think that I know
about her boyfriend but I overheard Aunt Coral talking
to Effie about him. She stopped when she saw me but I
think she really wanted me to hear.'

'She would, and I should hate to have to go to her
house so often, they're all so jolly odd aren't they? Lally's

just the same at school you know. She seems to think she's a walking occasion of sin and always owns up to something before the question's even been asked. If she says she's been talking she gets other people into trouble as well as she had to be talking to someone. Do you like having to be her friend?'

Gerry waited for an answer and Dorcas shrugged her shoulders. At last she said, 'Doesn't worry me and besides ...'

'What?'

'I think,' Dorcas said slowly, 'that Aunt Coral's nicer to Lally when I'm there. I don't really care if she's horrible to me because I can come home and forget about it but Lally's just got Effie and she's only tenpence-to-the-shilling, Mummy says.'

'Yes. Certainly no more than tenpence ha'penny.' Gerry picked up an out-of-date copy of *Woman's Weekly* and turned to the back page.

'Has your mother said anything about ... you know ... Mummy's boyfriend?'

'Listen to this.' Gerry's voice became nasal and constrained. '*I am soon to be married and as I have no mother nor close female relative to whom I can turn for advice I would be obliged if any of your readers could recommend a book or two I might purchase as I wish to be prepared in every way to be a good wife to my new husband. Anxious, Bridlington.*' Do you suppose,' Gerry said, 'that Anxious Bridlington is a place like Hazelbury Bryan or Sodding Chipbury where my grandmother lives?'

'Sodding Chipbury?'

'Chipping Sodbury. Or Indian Queens.' Dorcas was diverted and her question went unanswered as Gerry, older by two years and far older in experience, had intended. The two girls talked and read and made sorties to the kitchen for squash and biscuits as the afternoon passed from that state of anticipation of hours to be enjoyed that follows a busy morning into the pleasant but unproductive monotony of a wet afternoon, that condition of satisfactory boredom of which, in retrospect, childhood seems so full. When Alma returned to the house in Dobells Path she found Dorcas and Gerry in the front room sifting through a pile of old magazines, cutting out pictures and articles to stick into Dorcas's scrapbook.

Alma flicked on the light in the kitchen and propped her dripping umbrella in the sink before putting on the kettle and unwrapping the three lamb chops she had bought for the evening meal. 'Had a good day, you two?' She found old potatoes, rather green and full of sprouting eyes and started to peel them, talking to Gerry who had come into the kitchen and stood watching her.

'I've enjoyed myself very much, Mrs Westley. Mrs Westley, do you think Dorcas could come to our house next Saturday? If it's not too wet we could ride and if it does rain we'll find something to do. There are piles of old games and I've promised my mother that I'll help her sort out her books and she'll probably let us cook if we want to.'

The kitchen smelled faintly of gas, as it always did when the wind veered from its usual south-westerly course. The window was starting to haze with condensation and a message Dorcas had printed on the glass stood out, each letter expanding and dissolving but still clear enough to read. *I LOVE YOU. D. XX.*

Alma looked at Gerry and smiled. 'I'm quite sure Dorcas'd love to come to you but she's always gone to her friend Lally on a Saturday, you see, and I don't want to make things difficult.' Alma stopped, hands in the bowl of muddy water. 'You're a bit older than Dorcas aren't you Gerry, and I think you understand what I'm trying to say. How about if Dorcas goes to your house in a couple of weeks and I sort it out with Coral before then?' A look of understanding passed between them and Gerry went to collect her raincoat from the hall and to check that the return half of her bus ticket was still in the pocket under her gloves.

'Just walking to the bus stop with Gerry, Mum, won't be long.'

'Don't dawdle on the way back, Dorcas, there's someone coming to tea I want you to meet.' Alma closed the front door behind the girls and went back to the kitchen. She fetched a tin of pear halves from her emergency supply and transferred the quarter-pound of clotted cream she had bought into a glass dish before laying the table with a seersucker cloth and three clean napkins. She found two of her better glasses and Dorcas's mug but changed her mind and gave Dorcas a glass to match her own and Vernon's.

Alma wanted Dorcas back before Vernon Orme arrived; to talk to her, to introduce the thought of a third person infiltrating their twinned existence. She wished now that she had allowed Vernon to become familiar to Dorcas in a more casual way; that she had taken his advice and enabled a leisurely acquaintance to grow into familiarity, even fondness, between them, but the chance that Vernon had been waiting for had presented itself so unexpectedly that Alma had been caught almost unprepared by his proposal of marriage.

Everything was ready for the meal and Alma poured herself a second cup of tea and took it into the only other room on the ground floor of the little house. Dorcas's scrapbook was on the table between the armchairs and Alma skimmed through it. It was an eclectic mixture of pictures which appealed to Dorcas and which afforded Alma confused amusement.

There were advertisements for bird seed and pipe tobacco and rubber soles to prolong the life of shoes, pasted next to the whole of a Sunday evening's listening on the Third Programme as printed in the *Radio Times*. There were several of these listings but, as far as Alma knew, Dorcas had never even heard the Third Programme. Ballet dancers posed next to cricketers – a lot of these, suave but reliable and with tidy hair – and a series of the Kings and Queens of England, cut out with a wavy edge surrounding them like some attempt at a frame. There were cartoons and film stars smiling from the dusky pink paper of the popular fan magazine Alma sometimes brought home with her and, what Alma found most puzzling of all, application forms for samples of patent medicines.

The only real colour in the collection was from the Christmas and birthday cards all carefully stuck down with flour and water paste in the ledger old Mrs Westley had given Dorcas in which to draw, in the days when Roy was still alive and took his family to tea with his mother and sisters on every third Sunday of the month. Roy had drawn in the front of the book to amuse a small Dorcas and Alma felt apprehension tightening her throat as she looked at the familiar portraits. All the bodies were of stick men and women but the faces were carefully depicted, each a member of the family and each quite recognisable. Roy still smiled out at her, curly hair and crooked nose, alive with energy. Alma closed the book, turning it face downwards as if to imprison the memories it contained and as she did so she heard the front door open and laughter in the hall.

'Found this little drowned rat on the doorstep, says she lives here. Anything to do with you, is she?'

Dorcas looked at her mother, peering around the bulk that was Vernon Orme. There was something in the way that he held his head tilted backwards so that he looked down along the length of his nose that reminded Dorcas of a kangaroo. His legs, too, seemed exceptionally long as if to support the extra weight of his lower body and Dorcas would not have been altogether surprised to see him move in leaps and shuffles instead of the steady progress he was making as he swept her along in front of him. Alma came forward to take Dorcas's raincoat and Vernon put an arm around her and kissed her on the cheek, water scattering from him like silver baubles from a broken thermometer to land on the patterned linoleum that covered the hall floor.

'Give me your coat, Vernon. I'll hang them both over the bath and, Dorcas, fetch a cloth and mop the floor, there's a good girl.' Dorcas slid out of her shoes without untying the laces, knowing that Alma was too distracted to notice this forbidden practice. Vernon's observant kangaroo eyes watched Dorcas from a long way above her head. He saw that she was unlike her mother and where Alma was neat and quick in her movements, Dorcas was deliberate. Her hands were already bigger than Alma's but well shaped, bony, with square nails that were filed short, not left dirty and irregular in a way that he had always found disagreeable.

As Dorcas knelt at his feet with the floorcloth her heavy dark pigtails fell forwards and Vernon was aware of the absolutely straight pink parting that ran from the front of Dorcas's hair to the back. It was as if a channel had been marked out and a delta formed where the hair dispersed and was reclaimed again into two thick braids. Later in the year the sun would burn Dorcas's parting to a brown as dark as earth but now something about the uncompromising exposure of the child at his feet touched

Vernon and he understood at once that in his marriage to Alma he would have to accept a position of lesser importance to her than that of the child mopping rain from the floor. If he wavered it was only for a moment and he put out a hand to help Dorcas to her feet.

'Lucky we met like that, but we haven't been properly introduced. I'm Vernon Avery Orme, and you, I presume, are Miss Dorcas Westley. How do you do, Miss Westley?'

'How do you do, Mr Orme.' Dorcas's hand was still damp from the cloth she had been using but Vernon didn't seem to notice. He took her hand, shook it firmly and Dorcas was caught in the amiability of his smile, entangled in the web of his integrity. Alma coming downstairs in a clean frock and with her hair hastily brushed saw them disappearing together towards the kitchen, Dorcas still talking.

Alma had few doubts about Vernon's suitability as a husband but she needed Dorcas's approval. From the time she was a small child Dorcas had shown an unerring instinct about people and Alma had learned to take notice of what Dorcas thought. She still remembered with distaste Dorcas screaming and struggling to remove herself from the embrace of a schoolfriend of Roy's and the inexplicable friendship the child had established with an old and unlovely couple who spent most afternoons in a shelter on the promenade.

Roy's schoolfriend was now being held in a secure hospital with no date set for his release and the old couple had been found clasped together in death in the holiday flat that they had rented for the winter. Their possessions were so few it was as if they needed to leave nothing behind them except a small reminder that they had lived lives other than those circumscribed by the shabby flat and the windswept promenade. There were photographs of a woman with a sweet, serene face, her arm around a dark-skinned toddler wedged on her hip, a paler child holding her other hand and all three standing beside a young man in clerical black, smiling into the sun as he held a little girl in his arms. There were medals too, and letters written during the war, some of which had been quoted in the newspaper after the inquest on their death. The words had brought tears to Alma's eyes when she had read them, rising like little fish into her mind over the years on the singular occasions when she was feeling despondent.

Now Alma needed Dorcas to like Vernon. When he had asked Alma to marry him she had hesitated, not because she was unsure of her own feelings but because of Dorcas. She knew that her daughter's memory of Roy was fading although his photograph in a shagreen frame stood on Dorcas's chest of drawers and on his birthday and at Christmas and Easter they went together to the cemetery, up past the hospital and the playing fields, to the part of Penalverne where Alma and Coral had grown up.

On Roy's birthday, after they had changed the flowers in the sunken jam jar on his grave, Alma and

Dorcas would walk to the house where his mother lived and together with his sisters they would take tea with Mrs Westley. It was as if, by mutual agreement, this one day had been set aside to remember Roy and Dorcas listened, wide-eyed, to descriptions which changed by not so much as a word over the years, of a man she could no longer recognise as the father she had known.

Aunt Myrtle, of whom Dorcas was more than a little afraid, poured the tea and passed around dry heavy-cake. She asked Dorcas about school, testing her spelling and her mathematics, looking, Dorcas always thought, like a fatter version of the witch in *The Wizard of Oz*. Dorcas wondered whether Aunt Myrtle would dissolve with terrible cries into a puddle on the carpet if she flicked water at her but decided, after a look from Alma who seemed to know what she was thinking, not to try.

Aunt Minnie, even taller and heavier than her sister, seemed always to be hiding some secret mirth that might overwhelm good manners at an inopportune moment. Her eyes were as black as Myrtle's and her upper lip was covered in soft, dark hairs. Alma always waited in cold trepidation, willing Dorcas not to mention her aunt's moustache but Dorcas sat quietly in a corner reading a comic which Minnie had bought especially for her and seemed not to notice. They escaped as soon as they could and Alma always bought fish and chips on the way home as a treat.

Alma knew that she would never love Vernon as she had loved Roy but she had come to understand that such youthful, headlong infatuation might not have lasted as the demands of maturity encroached on their lives. Vernon was a good man, a widower, who loved Alma and was prepared to accept what she could offer him. He believed that in time she would grow to love him unconditionally and if this ambition was never quite fulfilled, Vernon never knew for Alma honoured her part of their bargain, caring for him tenderly and keeping secret any little disappointment that presented itself from time to time and which might have undermined the otherwise satisfactory tenor of their life together.

The chops that Alma was cooking for their tea were not large but sweet, and instead of the hasty mashing she usually afforded the potatoes she had added a knob of margarine and a splash of milk to the saucepan and had handed the bent kitchen fork to Vernon as if it were the most natural thing in the world, while she chopped the cabbage and made gravy in the frying pan. Dorcas liked her mother's gravy; it was thick and dark and salty and she dribbled it across her potatoes, criss-crossing the cabbage, aware that Vernon Orme was watching her but unhurried in her movements.

'Pass the mint sauce to Vernon, Dorcas.' Alma's voice was contained as if she were preparing to allow Dorcas to explain some trespass she had committed, but which explanation she was not altogether prepared to accept. Dorcas heard it and looked at her mother, searching her conscience but mindful that Alma was unsettled, uneasiness an unseen presence as if it were occupying the empty chair at the table, making up a foursome waiting for some intricate game to begin.

Dorcas pushed the jar of mint sauce on its saucer towards Vernon without looking at him and Alma said sharply, 'Dorcas!'

'Sorry. Would you like the mint sauce, Mr Orme?'

'Thank you, Miss Westley, but I prefer to taste my chop unalloyed.' Dorcas looked at Vernon and he winked one kangaroo eye at her. 'Got to watch the old tum these days; vinegar's out, I'm sorry to say.'

'I don't like it either. Mr Orme?'

'Yes, Miss Westley.'

'Why don't you call me Dorcas like everybody else does?'

'Would you prefer that I did?'

'Of course.'

'Well then, I will – on condition that you call me Uncle Vernon.'

Dorcas looked at him consideringly, noticing for the first time that his skin was tight and shiny and covered with large freckles. She shook her head.

'No?'

'No, but I could just call you Vernon, if you like.'

Vernon put out a restraining hand to Alma without looking in her direction and smiled at Dorcas. 'I call that an acceptable bargain. We should shake on it.' He spat on his palm and held out his hand to Dorcas. She hesitated, then spat vigorously on her own palm and held it out to him.

'Honestly, Vernon, whatever are you teaching my daughter?' The man and the child both laughed and Alma joined in, unaware of the affiliation which had just been negotiated and agreed without her involvement.

Dorcas concentrated on forming a volcano of mashed potato, gravy lava trickling down breaches she was making in the rim of the crater, so she missed altogether the look exchanged between Alma and Vernon. Alma had replied with a shake of the head to Vernon's unspoken question and the atmosphere around the table, lightened for a while, returned to its former friendly silence while they finished eating. Dorcas, at a word from her mother, collected the empty plates and made an unsteady pile of them on the draining-board, carrying to the table pudding bowls and the pears and cream. She allowed the thick, crusty cream to slide slowly off the special flat-edged spoon onto her fruit and took tiny mouthfuls of the gritty, sweet flesh to prolong her enjoyment. Tinned pears were her favourite and the smallest size she and her mother usually shared didn't go far between three. She was surprised when a spoon with a quarter of a pear in it hovered over her bowl as Alma passed some of her share to Dorcas. Dorcas looked up with a smile and waited, knowing that Alma had something to say.

'We, Vernon and I that is, wondered if you'd like to come out for a drive with us tomorrow? We thought we'd go and have a look at a house that he's thinking of buying. It sounds really lovely and he says that he'd value our opinion of it. What d'you think, Dorcas?'

'OK.' Dorcas shrugged her shoulders. 'Is it far?'

There was the slightest hesitation and then Alma said, 'It's in Devon, so we'll leave early and take a picnic; you know how you love a picnic.' Her voice was almost wheedling, 'It's near the coast and the beaches are all sandy, not pebbles like here. Ideal, really.'

It wasn't until Dorcas was lying in bed listening to her mother and Vernon laughing together at something on the wireless, that she wondered why it should matter to Vernon whether or not she liked his house, and what had her mother meant by saying that the beach was ideal. Ideal for what?

Dorcas's dreams were always vivid and now, when she fell asleep, kangaroos leapt through her mind, heavy legs and tails thumping on an ideal sandy beach. The oldest and largest of the animals was smoking a pipe of Three Nuns tobacco which he extinguished with a wink before accepting from Dorcas a corned beef sandwich and a saffron bun. She offered him a drink of her cherryade but from somewhere bottles of light ale had appeared and the kangaroo passed them around to his friends, handing one to a shadowy figure who sat just out of Dorcas's sight on the old army blanket that Alma kept especially for picnics. Dorcas couldn't see her mother anywhere but she was not concerned and slept deeply, surrounded by her marsupial companions, who gathered the empty bottles and greaseproof bags and uneaten apple cores, tidying them away into their pouches before springing and bounding out of sight along the wide, sea-damp beach.

When Dorcas woke it was to the sound of more rain. The gutter above her bedroom was broken and a drip sounded rhythmically on the lid of the dustbin which stood in the yard below her window. She lay quietly for a little while, trying to recapture the feeling of contentment in her dream; nearly but never quite entangling reality and illusion in a way which would persist long enough for her to carry it through the day like some brittle bone which had been entrusted to her and which she must preserve from breaking for as long as she could. Dorcas knew that the memories of the night would shiver gently to pieces as the day grew older so that by the time that Vernon came to collect her and Alma nothing would be left except an image like an elusive shadow seen out of the corner of her eye.

'Wakey-wakey!' Alma pushed open the door of Dorcas's bedroom. 'Still raining so we'll just have to make the best of it. Better take an extra jersey and we'll put your wellington boots in Vernon's car.' She sat down suddenly on the foot of the bed and Dorcas drew her legs out of the way. 'What did you think of Vernon then? He took to you at once, I could see that, and you seemed to have plenty to say to him, which surprised me as you're usually so quiet with people you don't know.'

'He's all right.' Dorcas's eyes were full of some emotion with which Alma was unfamiliar.

'Just all right?'

'Very nice.' Dorcas smiled. 'I thought he looked like a kangaroo.'

Alma studied her daughter, tangled dark hair and shoulders already broad for a child. 'You're absolutely right. I'd never have thought of it myself but I can see just what you mean. It's his shape, isn't it?'

'And his eyes. They're kind but quite penetrating, don't you think?'

'You are a funny child, Dorcas. Where *do* you learn these expressions?' Alma got up and walked the two steps that separated Dorcas's bed from her wardrobe, taking out from the cupboard a pair of thick trousers which she laid on the bed. 'Better wear these, it's not that warm.' She hesitated and then continued in a different tone of voice, one to which Dorcas was unaccustomed. 'You do *like* Vernon, though, don't you?'

'Are you going to marry him?'

Alma sat down again. 'Would you mind if I did? He has asked me but I can only marry him if you agree too.'

'And this house in Devon we're going to see, is it where we'd have to live?' Dorcas thought of the house she saw so often in her dreams, of its quietness and the garden and the river that was an essential part of it.

'It's not just an ordinary house like this one, Dorcas. It's very old and quite big and Vernon's got a chance to buy it and he thought that he and I could run it together as a hotel.'

Dorcas turned her head towards the photograph of her father, segregated and solitary in his green leather frame, and felt tears stinging her eyes. Alma saw them and put out a hand towards the child but Dorcas evaded her touch, wiping her cheeks with a corner of the sheet and trying to smile. 'I don't mind if that's what you want. Vernon's OK but I don't want to change my name. Can I still be Dorcas Westley?'

'Of course, if that's what will make you happy although Vernon would be quite pleased if you took his name. In fact, I think he'd like it very much, but it's up to you.' Alma hesitated, 'He has a daughter too, you know. She's called Hilary and she lives in Canada.'

Dorcas's eyes, still bright with tears, seemed to fill with sorrow: she understood the pain of separation. 'Well, as I haven't got a father and Vernon's daughter's so far away . . . Do you think that Daddy would mind?'

Alma shook her head. 'I didn't mean to spring it on you like this, but we have to decide quickly about buying Petty Place.'

'It's OK. Anyway, I knew about Vernon already, I heard Aunt Coral talking about him to Effie. But not about Hilary,' she said slowly. 'Mummy?'

'Yes?'

'Why does Hilary live in Canada?'

'A lot of children were sent to Canada at the beginning of the war, to get them out of danger.' Alma played with a thread that had worked itself loose from one of the patches that made up the quilt that covered Dorcas's bed. Two little Scottie dogs, one black and one white on a red background, and a navy and white spotted cotton, a reminder of the dresses she and Dorcas had worn that last summer when they were all together as a family. 'Vernon's wife died when Hilary was very small and his parents looked after her most of the time but when the war started they all decided together that she should go to her aunt in Canada. Her aunt is Vernon's sister and she has three children of her own so they felt that Hilary would be happy there.' Alma's hand strayed to a patch of blue-and-white poplin, a piece taken from the tail of one of Roy's shirts. 'A blessing as it turned out as the Ormes' house in Plymouth took a direct hit and they were both killed one night when the German planes were bombing the docks.'

Dorcas thought about this. 'But why didn't Hilary come back after the war?'

'Well, I suppose she'd settled out there by then: you see Vernon couldn't get to see her for years while the war was on and when he did manage to go last year he said that she hardly recognised him. He'd expected her to sound English, just like she did before she went away, but of course she didn't. She's got a Canadian accent and a Canadian boyfriend — well, he's actually from Eastern Europe somewhere, with a funny sounding name that I can never remember — but he will be a Canadian when he's been naturalised.'

'So she's lost to him forever?'

Alma stopped picking at the thread and gave Dorcas a funny look. 'I wouldn't go as far as that. You make it sound terribly dramatic but it isn't really like that at all. It's just a bit sad really and he does miss her

80

but he wants to do what's best for *her*. Do you understand?'

'I think so.' Alma, looking at Dorcas, realised how like Roy and his sisters she was growing, her thick, dark hair and sturdy body so unlike her own neat prettiness. Dorcas spoke again. 'I'll miss Lally if we move and there'll be no-one to look after her if I'm not there. I expect she'll come and stay though, won't she? If Aunt Coral's well enough not to need her all the time?'

The little bedroom was growing lighter and Alma drew back the curtains. The day was overcast, slate and granite slick as oil under the onslaught of the rain, grey gulls cruising silently inland, away from the choppy water and the agitation of waves collapsing on to the pebbles of the beach, drawing them back in the undertow to leave patches of bare sand and weed torn from underwater gardens. Until the next tide high enough to float it off the beach would be covered with seaweed; slimy, glutinous strands filling the air around with the smell of decomposition, flies rising in clouds at any slight disturbance. There were cuttlefish, too, strung along the wrack like elongated pearls in a necklace, and mermaids' purses, dead fish and driftwood, mashed and broken beyond recognition as a tree or a packing case or an oar.

Dorcas longed to walk along the rainy beach, dodging the incoming sea, collecting pebbles which lost their shine as soon as they were dry, and shells the colour of butter. She wondered if the ideal sandy beach would yield such treasure and slid reluctantly out of bed to pad the few steps along the landing to the bathroom.

'Hurry up, my lover, we're already all behind like the cow's tail with all that talking. I'll go and get your breakfast and you get dressed as quickly as you can and come and give me a hand with the sandwiches.' Alma stopped at the door of the bathroom to watch Dorcas cleaning her teeth. 'You don't need to worry about Lally you know. Uncle Billy will look after her – he's always thought the world of her. And there's Effie, and even Coral has to let Mary Marigold grow up at some time. Anyway, I expect we'll still see quite a bit of her. Now get a move on or Vernon will be here and we won't be ready.'

Dorcas sat in the back of Vernon's elderly Austin, the picnic basket on the seat beside her. The car was very hot, to keep the windscreen clear, Vernon explained and Dorcas's thick trousers prickled her legs, making her fidgety and uncomfortable. She had finished the bag of sherbet Alma had given her with instructions not to spill it all over the inside of Vernon's nice car. Dorcas looked at her finger, as yellow as that of a thirty-a-day smoker and wrinkled, where she had sucked the acid crystals from it. The sherbet had made her thirsty and she was bored.

The rain was relentless and from time to time she wiped her hand over the inside of the window, leaving a fan-shaped hole through which she tried to see where they were but everywhere looked the same: grey skies, grey houses, fields enveloped in grey mist. Even the trees seemed to have leached their colour into the leaden air and Dorcas sat back and closed her eyes.

When she opened them the rain had stopped and the earth in the dark fields she was used to had turned to red. Dorcas could see cows stained with wet, rusty-looking mud halfway up their flanks, their legs sleek and auburn among puddles the colour of stewed tea. Hills which had looked so dismal only a few hours ago were now green, their outline softened by evaporating mist as the sun struggled to shine. 'There,' Alma said, 'enough blue to make a sailor a pair of trousers. It's going to be a lovely day after all.' Vernon gave her a sideways look full of affection, and Dorcas turned hurriedly towards the window.

The long grass in the fields struggled to overcome clumps of nettles and the coppery stems of sorrel and in the hedges, between which they were now driving, there were moon daisies and bluebells and campion, and wild garlic scented the car when Dorcas wound down the window at Vernon's suggestion that she might see a rainbow. Cow parsley was thick along the verges of the road but its delicacy and sweetness gave way to the coarser yellow flowers of Alexanders as the car drew nearer to the coast.

'Not far now. All right in the back there?' Vernon looked in the rear-view mirror, catching Dorcas's gaze before she had time to allow her eyes to evade his.

'Yes, thank you, but I'm starving hungry.'

'We'll have our picnic as soon as we stop. Oh, Dorcas, isn't it pretty here? All these little lanes full of flowers and the hills so round and green. It all seems so much softer somehow, so . . .' Alma searched for the word that would encompass this new landscape. 'So . . . comfortable.'

Dorcas didn't bother to answer. She thought of the gorse bushes which scratched her legs and the blue butterflies, no bigger than her thumbnail, which darted and fluttered among the moss and wild roses on the wall around the house in Hobba Woods: a house declined and empty but where she and Lally sometimes played among the palm trees, which grew ragged and primitive among abandoned flower beds. They never went into the house itself but sat under the magnolia bushes or hollowed out a space in the stands of bamboo, where they stored the flower heads and seeds that they collected from plants which were gradually encroaching on the pebbled paths. Lawns, too, were still discernible but were no longer a smooth emerald; now they were starred with daisies and Scarlet Pimpernel and tiny blue birdseye.

Behind the house there was a pond, the water as green as the grass and nearly as impenetrable, but dragonflies and damselflies hovered over it, wings glinting in the sun. Once, and Dorcas had to force herself to remember it, they had seen an adder asleep in the sun, its zig-zag back a sinuous curve, the flat head resting on a loop of its own body. Dorcas had screamed, pretending to be more frightened than she was, and had run away but

Lally had lingered, looking at the snake's turquoise belly and creamy scales, wanting to see it move, to slither and slide and to insinuate itself back into the crack in the wall where it lived.

They never told anyone about the garden, nor about the time they had squatted down to pee behind a ceanothus bush as blue as the sky, modest even in that deserted place, and had seen a pair of eyes watching them, a pair of hands fiddling with trouser buttons. They had laughed and run off together, pulling up their knickers as they went. After that they played in Lally's garden for a while and when they went back to the house in Hobba Woods there was a wire fence around it and bulldozers were crushing the stones, tearing flowers and trees apart as easily as Dorcas and Lally did themselves when they made a garden of plasticine.

Vernon slowed almost to a stop at a junction in the lane. 'Close your eyes, Alma. You too, Dorcas, and don't open them until I say.' He turned on to what seemed to be a cart track, so insignificant that grass grew in the loose gravel that had been churned by passing wheels into a strip along the centre of the lane. When he was certain that his passengers had done as he asked, he turned left again and allowed the car to cruise gently downhill for about a quarter of a mile before stopping almost imperceptibly. 'You can open them now.'

They were parked by a triangle of grass where the lane they had driven along was bisected by one even narrower, the two merging and widening as it turned a corner just ahead. The sea seemed to lap against the foot of the cliff below them, glittering and swaying in the light of the newly emerged sun, as a rim of lemon-coloured sand showed with each withdrawn wave, leaving sand bars and ledges of rock suspended in a shimmering, colourless sea.

Ahead of them, half hidden by a fold in the hill, was a house just as Dorcas had imagined it, plain and grey with large windows set one above the other reaching almost to the roof which, from this perspective, appeared to be flat. It looked like a child's drawing, square and unadorned, but as they drew nearer banks of chimney pots emerged, twisted bricks, coloured and patterned, as if the lack of ornament on the house itself had erupted above the house like a shower of fireworks, revealed only to those who came close enough to see.

Dorcas was out of the car almost before it had stopped and was standing looking at the peeling front door by the time that Vernon and Alma joined her. 'We have to wait for Mr Brompton to meet us here with the key but he shouldn't be long.'

Dorcas was afraid to look away in case the house dissolved as it always did in her dream. She had to hold it steady by the force of her mind, to be able to open the door and walk into the cool, quiet rooms and up the staircase which she knew would face the front door and which would divide into two on the first landing. It was here in her dream that Dorcas always woke up, never having decided which branch of the staircase she should follow, but knowing that it was so important that one day the choice would be forced upon her.

Dorcas's dream had started soon after her father had died. It had become habitual, an old friend, so that even in sleep she would recognise features already revealed and take herself in imagination to that place where she had left the dream on a previous occasion.

Dorcas looked again at the front of the house, so familiar but so perilously full of the unknown, at her mother and Vernon and Vernon's car, streaked with red mud from the rain they had driven through to get here. On either side of the front door was a column, neither of them absolutely straight, whose cushion capitals were roofed by a modest porch which projected over the front door. Their asymmetry added to the impression that the whole building had been constructed out of a child's imagination and gave Petty Place a charm that seduced even those who knew nothing about perfect proportions and the balance of fenestration. Dorcas counted fourteen windows, each with a rounded gable and a prominent keystone. The keystones reminded her of pineapple chunks, the chunk in the topmost row almost touching a cornice of what looked to Dorcas like a row of gappy teeth.

She turned towards her mother. 'It's just like the house in my dream and did you see all those horses we passed? Weren't they *lovely*?'

'I don't know about any horses,' Alma sounded doubtful,' but I did see bluebells in the woods, whole banks of them like an inland sea among the trees, and rhododendrons just coming out.'

A green sports car rounded the last bend in the drive and stopped very suddenly, scattering dust and small stones everywhere. A young man got out of the car. He was very tall and very fair with a hesitant moustache that had an unfortunate tendency to grow ginger if not kept under control.

'Ralph Brompton.' He took off a very new leather driving-glove and held out his hand to Vernon. 'You must be Mr Orme – how d'you do? What do you think of the old place then?'

'How do you do?' Vernon put his hand under Alma's elbow. 'May I introduce Mrs Westley and Miss Dorcas Westley?'

Ralph Brompton looked at Alma and Dorcas as if noticing them for the first time but he didn't shake their hands. 'Look, I'm awfully sorry but something's come up and much as I'd love to show you around, no can do I'm afraid. OK if I leave the key with you? Just lob it back into the office when you've finished but take as much time as you want.' Without waiting for an answer he thrust several keys on a chain towards Vernon, got into his car, backed it and drove off, more dust and more pebbles flying from beneath his tyres.

Vernon watched him go. 'Hope we can trust him,' he said. 'Saw a lot like that during the war, all talk and shiny shoes but no substance to them. We'd better make up our minds before he changes his and get things on a legal footing as soon as possible.' Dorcas's mouth was dry and Vernon, noticing how pale she was, said heartily, 'First things first, though. Picnic time, I fancy. You choose, Dorcas, inside or out?'

'I think there might be a little temple thing in the garden,' Dorcas said. 'Could we have our picnic there, do you think?'

Alma handed a rug to Dorcas and went on unloading the car. She picked up the basket which held flasks of tea for her and Vernon and a bottle of Corona cherryade for Dorcas. 'What makes you think that? Have you seen a picture of it – in your scrapbook, perhaps?'

Dorcas shook her head. 'I told you, it's the house in my dream. It's got a divided staircase and a dairy with green tiles and the temple and two little bridges.' She hooked her hand around the handle of the picnic basket to pull it over the leather seat towards the door of the car. 'Don't worry, it's a lucky house and people who live here are always happy.'

'Stop that, Dorcas. I've told you before about letting your imagination run away with you.' Alma's heart ached when she allowed herself to acknowledge that Dorcas filled the spaces in her life with intangibles; her dreams, her imaginary horses, but today was not the time to be indulgent and her voice sounded sharper than she intended. She added more gently, 'Vernon doesn't want to hear all your nonsense, not today at any rate, we've got a lot to get through.' But Vernon, picking up the basket of sandwiches and cake, smiled at Dorcas and led the small party through an archway covered in the straggly remains of Virginia creeper, some scarlet and brown leaves still clinging stubbornly to their vines.

They crossed a cobbled yard and went out through a lower arched gateway and there, stretching around them like an encircling cloth, were gardens and a stream crossed by two small bridges. On a rise to their right backed by dark hedges was, not a temple, but a little pagoda, its roofs painted red and gold, tiny dragons carved on each upturned corner. It shone in the pale air, just as Dorcas had always known that it would.

Later on, after Vernon had juggled with the keys on Ralph Brompton's chain, they had gone into the house and walked through the empty, beautiful, dusty rooms. Later still they had mounted the staircase three-abreast, their feet impatient on the wide bare boards. When they came to the landing where the stairs divided Dorcas hesitated for only a moment before following Vernon up the left-hand side while Alma walked on alone to the right.

CHAPTER FIVE

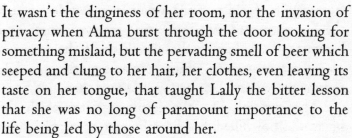

It wasn't the dinginess of her room, nor the invasion of privacy when Alma burst through the door looking for something mislaid, but the pervading smell of beer which seeped and clung to her hair, her clothes, even leaving its taste on her tongue, that taught Lally the bitter lesson that she was no long of paramount importance to the life being led by those around her.

It wasn't that Alma or Vernon was unkind; on the contrary, they cared for Lally with exactly the same relaxed concern with which they treated Dorcas but Lally was not used to such perceived indifference and hardly knew how to respond. The room she had been given this time was on a mezzanine floor above the kitchen, hardly more than a boxroom, where over-sized dishes were stored, linen awaiting mending, cake stands and artificial flowers.

Every year since Vernon and Alma had married

and moved to Petty Place, the Bassetts had visited
them for two weeks in the autumn, returning to the
house in Advent Gardens in time for the start of the
Christmas term at St Perpetua's. Lally often stayed on
her own at Petty Place, in a room that overlooked the
cobbled courtyard and had the faint gingery smell of all
old bedrooms; a lingering echo of brilliantined young
men and girls with swansdown powder puffs, of Marie
biscuits and the not quite extinguished dampness of croup
kettles that even two coats of pale pink emulsion could
not altogether eliminate.

Dorcas had painted the walls and had appropriated
from a pile of old curtains a pair in rose velvet which
she had shortened, not by cutting them to length and
hemming them, but by the expedient of the insertion
of a great many pins which grew rusty and immobile
as time passed and Dorcas forgot about them.

The curtains, like the furniture with which the
house was now filled, had been bought at local auctions
by Vernon, heavy old-fashioned pieces, too large for
the post-war houses that a lot of people were now
equipping. He chose only what appealed to him and had
the unforeseen satisfaction of watching his investment
steadily increasing in value over the years.

From the first Petty Place had flourished, word-of-
mouth ensuring that in every season of the year the hotel
was as full as it needed to be and in the summer holidays
and at Christmas there was never an empty room.

After taking Vernon's advice Alma had asked Mrs

Westley to visit them and twice she and her daughters had come to stay at Petty Place in the lull after Christmas and the New Year. The rhododendrons had been out, the ash trees hazing into tender green, but the country hadn't suited them and only Myrtle had made the journey from Penalverne once more before agreeing that Dorcas was no longer the child they knew, their brother's daughter cast in their exact mould, but who had grown away from them.

The Westleys tried to disapprove of Vernon but found nothing but kindness and conviviality in his manner towards them, Minnie, inevitably, becoming girlish and arch when he spoke to her, Myrtle remaining obstinately unimpressed by Alma's rise in fortune. They reverted to writing to Dorcas at Christmas and Easter and tried not to mind when Roy's birthday passed unremembered.

The Westleys had visited Petty Place in the quiet days of early spring but Billy and Coral Bassett took their holiday in the late summer and it was Vernon who had diffused a difficult situation at the end of their first visit by treating as a joke Coral's assumption that they would receive both a late season discount and a further reduction as friends of long standing. The summer following this awkwardness, however, saw the older Bassetts going to Capri although by Christmas they thought that Lally would enjoy being with Dorcas again and paid their account without argument, knowing that they were lucky to be accommodated at all.

That was the happiest Christmas that Effie had ever known. She had sung and chortled all day long, helping the two girls to decorate the Christmas tree which stood in a corner of the hall, discovering an untried ability to make spectacular garlands which she wound around the bannisters, draping holly and ivy over every available support until Vernon had muttered to Alma that he half expected, not Father Christmas, but Tarzan to come swinging through the greenery. Effie made herself useful in the kitchens, often not being immediately available to Coral, who became fretful and peevish as she searched through room after room, Effie managing to remain out of the way for as long as she chose.

Before they returned to Advent Gardens Vernon had given Effie an envelope. 'Wages, Effie, we couldn't have managed without you. It's not a cheque,' he said, noticing that she looked anxious. 'It's cash, so that no-one else need know and any time you want a job . . .' He smiled and gave her a peck on the cheek and Effie slid the envelope into the pocket of her pinafore thinking that Mr Orme really was a lovely man.

In her makeshift bedroom Lally sat on the edge of the bed and wondered how things could have gone so wrong. She looked forward to her summer holiday at Petty Place all through the year and although Alma and Vernon had been as welcoming as ever and Dorcas seemed pleased to see her, it was Gerry Jarvie who was sleeping on a

Z-bed in Dorcas's bedroom and Lally who had been exiled to this hot, smelly little room where the sounds of a busy kitchen were faintly audible beneath her late into the night and where the smell of stale drink seemed to insinuate itself through the floorboards, enveloping and choking her. Alma had been apologetic but explained that she thought of Lally as family and that the family sometimes had to take second place to guests who paid for their accommodation and that she knew Lally would understand. Lally understood very well and was shamed by the knowledge; angry, not with her mother, but with Alma who allowed Coral to take advantage of their long friendship.

The Bassetts had been as surprised as anyone to discover that Petty Place belonged to the Jarvies: not to Gerry's father, but to his elder brother, whose family lived at the home farm and who had been delighted to find someone willing to buy the house. They had neither the time nor the inclination to try to reverse the neglect that had begun its inevitable incursion on the fabric once the ballet school which had occupied Petty Place during the war had returned to London. In spite of their unwillingness to spend money on its upkeep themselves, the Jarvies had a sentimental attachment to the house and it was Frances Jarvie, Gerry's mother, who had persuaded them that Vernon Orme would be the ideal custodian of what they continued to think of as their own property. Apart from very minor alterations and the installation of several bathrooms Vernon had allowed the house to dictate the way in which the hotel was run, but its atmosphere of harmony and cheerfulness was due directly to Alma and to Vernon himself.

Gerry had arrived before Lally and, by now established custom, had taken the extra bed in Dorcas's room. By the time Lally joined them a few days later a pattern of habit had already been established and she detected an unexpected note of indifference in Dorcas's voice if any reservation were expressed by Lally about the plan advanced for their entertainment. It wasn't until the wedding reception, though, that Lally truly realised that her misgivings had a basis of truth.

'Backyard trots, my foot.' Alma put down the phone. 'All three of them! I should have known we'd have trouble with the Fair in town. What *am* I to do?' It was breakfast time and the girls were eating toast, standing about in everyone's way, shifting and reforming as the preparations for the wedding reception surged around them.

'No problem, Mrs O, we'll be your waitresses,' Gerry said through a mouthful of toast and honey. 'I quite fancy myself in black stockings and a white pinny.' She wiggled her hips.

'Oh, Gerry, I couldn't allow that. Whatever would your mother say? But thank you for the offer all the same.'

'Mum wouldn't mind, honestly.'

'Go on, Mummy. *Please* let us.'

Alma looked at Lally. 'What about you, Lally? Coral wouldn't be happy about it, I know that, but perhaps you could work in the kitchen and then one of the other girls could waitress instead.'

'If that's what would help you, I'd be happy to do it,' Lally said, her smile deluding Alma, concealing the resentful words that Lally would have spoken if she had listened to the voice inside her head.

Alma made a little face at Dorcas. 'You're angels, you've absolutely saved my life. Now, you don't need to get ready until about two o'clock; the uniforms are in the wardrobe in Lally's room and some stockings should be in a box in there as well. Do your best with them, the other girls will help you. And, Lally, you can start work when you like — just a white apron. Oh, and I'd wear old shoes if I were you.'

Lally had no old shoes and afraid of what her mother would say if she went home with grease on the new black suede that Coral had insisted on lending her, she borrowed a pair from Dorcas, two sizes too big but safe enough with the laces tightly tied.

Dorcas and Gerry giggled and tugged themselves into two spare black dresses and helped each other into the starched organdie pinafores that they wore over them, straightening the straps which criss-crossed at the back. Dorcas's hair was already plaited and pinned around her head but Gerry's long red hair had to be subdued into tidiness before they could each put on the frilled head-dress that completed their transformation.

'We look like a mad sort of nun,' Dorcas said. 'Oh gosh, I can't laugh or I'll split the seams.'

'It does look a bit small, but just keep smiling and no-one'll notice. Aren't these stockings just *thrilling*?' Gerry pulled up her skirt and posed with a finger to her lips.

'You look like a maid in a French farce.'

'Shame, I hoped I looked like a tart.'

Dorcas laughed. 'Shush, you're shocking Lally.' She turned to her friend. 'Oh Lally, I wish you'd change your mind. Absolutely *everyone* is coming to the reception and it would be such fun if we were all together. Aunt Coral would never know. Won't you, please?'

Lally was shaken at this casual suggestion that she should deceive her mother and looked at Dorcas in the borrowed dress which was too short and too tight; at her rather heavy legs in flat, sensible shoes and at the stiff broderie anglaise head-dress held on by kirby grips, and she thought how awful Dorcas looked and how much she envied her.

Lally shook her head. 'I really don't mind being in the kitchen – I can't make a mess of washing-up, can I? I'd be sure to drop something if I was serving and I don't know anything about drinks.' Years of dissimulation had left Lally a mistress in the art and not even Dorcas suspected that she was speaking anything but the truth.

'All you have to do is to smile and make a joke of it; nobody will think you're *actually* a waitress, for goodness sake.' Gerry's voice with its faint, unplaceable accent, sounded irritated. Lally said nothing but gave a half-smile. She would never allow this intruder with her confident assumptions to shake her resolution.

'We'll try and smuggle some champagne out to you. Oh,' Dorcas stopped. 'I'd forgotten. You don't drink any more, do you? Never mind, we'll think of something.'

Gerry, more perspicacious than Lally had believed, looked sideways at Dorcas and then said casually, 'Eugene will be there, of course. Perhaps we could smuggle him out to Lally, because if I'm not mistaken my cousin made a bit of an impression last time they met.'

Lally bent down to re-tie the laces on the huge shoes that Dorcas had lent her. Anything, anything, to hide her face, to camouflage the blush she felt rising from the pit of her stomach and which she knew would betray the depth of her longing to see Eugene Jarvie again. When she could temporise no longer she looked up to see Gerry watching her and knew that her diversion had been in vain. Gerry laughed and Lally thought how nice it would be to hurt her so much that she couldn't laugh at her ever again. 'Thought so, you naughty old thing. What *would* Mother Scholastica say if she knew that her model pupil had sinful thoughts about a young man who, even yet, might be saved for the priesthood?'

Lally's mouth was dry. 'Is . . . is your cousin going to be a priest?' *Don't say his name, don't speak it aloud. It's only to be said in secret, softly, coupled with your own — Lally and Eugene. Eugene and Lally Jarvie.* 'I didn't know, no-one told me.'

'Honestly, Lally! Of course he's not; can you *imagine* anyone less suitable than Eugene?' Gerry's voice was amused. 'Besides, he's currently being pursued by all the unmarried women in two counties. *And* some of the only temporarily unmarried – you know, the ones who are single just for the afternoon or a weekend – but he doesn't seem overly bothered about any of them.'

'You don't mean . . . ?' Dorcas, newly knowledgeable, didn't finish the sentence.

'Nothing like that. No, he's masculine all right but he's had girls after him ever since his voice broke and he doesn't seem to have to try like anyone else. Actually, he hardly seems to notice them much of the time.'

Lally listened to Gerry, only half understanding what she was saying, conscious of a dread deep inside her that Eugene would choose her from among all the others and that she would have to decide whether to succumb to her own desire for him and be plunged into mortal sin, or whether she could resist and save both their souls. Mother Mary John had told her that a good Catholic girl, by allowing herself to give her company to a man intent on drink or seduction, might save him from himself but Lally thought that what she had in mind for Eugene's deliverance would not have been covered by Mother Mary John's advice.

She started a prayer to Our Lady for guidance and strength and only half heard Dorcas's laughing assertion that Eugene Jarvie wouldn't need to ask *her* twice. Dorcas and Gerry were sharing the Max Factor Crème Puff and a peachy lipstick which suited them both while Lally looked with distaste at the grubby cotton wool which they used indiscriminately, each in turn. Dorcas opened a little silk bag in which she kept her make-up, took out a block of mascara and spat on it before scrubbing a brush around and coating her eyelashes. She passed it to Gerry, who repeated the performance as Lally watched, repelled. She was aware that Gerry had an only half-stifled desire to shock and that Dorcas was becoming more and more like her. No, Lally thought, it was more than that: Dorcas had already become like Gerry, or perhaps it was that they had always been alike, Dorcas needing only confidence to step forward and take her place among those who lived their life free from the fear of censure.

Vernon had been happy to pay for Dorcas to go as a weekly boarder to a school in Exeter and he encouraged her to make the most of the opportunities this afforded of widening her circle of friends. His concern was mainly altruistic although he was aware that Dorcas's slightly old-fashioned demeanour and unaffected manners reflected well on her home life and thus of Petty Place. Vernon was pleased that Dorcas's friendship with Gerry had developed and although he understood her continuing loyalty to Lally he acknowledged a growing misgiving that Lally's submission, understandable in a child, was becoming disquieting. When he spoke to Alma about her, Alma laughed and said that Lally always had been an odd little creature, full of Coral's crackpot ideas and oppressed by her religion and not to worry as she had all her buttons done up the right way really.

After this, Vernon thought better of mentioning to

Alma the way in which Lally would stand posing in front of her mirror with the door of her bedroom half open when she knew that Vernon was upstairs on his own. There was no attempt at concealment and Vernon felt uncomfortably certain that there was every intention to entrap. Nor did Vernon mention, for fear of seeming to be over preoccupied with Lally, that a pair of cufflinks which he had been given by his father had disappeared, although he knew without doubt that he had left them on top of the tallboy in the room that he shared with Alma.

Vernon tried to ensure that he was never left alone with Lally and became hearty and jocular when speaking to her. She had become very beautiful in a subdued and delicate way, as if she had discarded a skin somewhere along the years and now needed to be treated with circumspection in case her lack of adequate protection should allow the normal incursions of daily life to graze her flesh and bruise her spirit.

Alma, busier than she had ever been, made the mistake of not taking seriously Lally's sensitivity, believing her to be just as she had been at six or twelve, and treating her as she had treated her then, with an exasperated acceptance. Where once Alma had always thought of Dorcas and Lally together, she had noticed that it was now Dorcas and Gerry, Lally being acknowledged as the third element of the friendship.

There was, too, a fourth component of which Alma was still only vaguely aware. Eugene Jarvie was Gerry's cousin, a young man of such comeliness and good looks that he was, as Gerry had pointed out, a danger to nearly every susceptible female with whom he came into contact. It would not be true, however, to accept Gerry's assertion that Eugene was entirely unaware of this effect but it seemed to him unimportant, a part of his make-up as unremarkable as his overlarge ears or the colour of his eyes.

Gerry often came to Devon in the holidays and divided her time between Petty Place and Home Farm, where her uncle and aunt treated her as one of their own, glad of her company as a companion to her aunt who was isolated in a household of men. They had accepted Dorcas as Gerry's friend, pleased by her old-fashioned manners and amused by the way she spoke in phrases taken from whatever book she happened to be reading at the time. They understood this to be her defence against the loneliness of an only child left alone for long periods of time, and unusually Dorcas, unlike many of the solitary, didn't lose her imposed silence when she was among other people. She remained reserved and self-contained, speaking little but listening to everything, both spoken and implied. She was, the Jarvies thought, the ideal foil to Gerry, and Dorcas, aware as she grew older of her privileged position, took every opportunity to move, almost unobserved, from the pitied object of Coral Bassett's condescension to being a young woman who was accepted without question as a friend of the Jarvies, wherever she chose to go.

Dorcas's upward progress may have been unnoticed by some but not by the family who still lived in Advent Gardens and who clung with such tenacity to a friendship which many would have regarded as spent. In the course of Dorcas's school career her voice had undergone that metamorphosis which Lally had been forced to endure in weekly elocution lessons. Her manners had become polished where, previously, they had been only pleasingly natural and her customary air of detachment lent an aspect which could be interpreted as that acquired from years of advantage.

Dorcas, always a solid, weighty-looking child, had grown into a young woman who gave promise of being handsome in middle age but whose features were too pronounced, too commanding, for her to be singled out as pretty. Her eyes were deeply set and secretive; her mouth, under a nose with a bend in it like her father's, was firm but reflected the amusement she saw in most things, and her hair was dark, black in some lights, almost mahogany in others. Dorcas could scarcely remember the last time she had been to the hairdresser, Alma trimming an inch or two off the length when it grew thin and straggly at the ends. Dorcas plaited it and wound the plait around the top of her head and, once done, she gave no more thought to her hair until she took it down at night, brushed it and tied it loosely into two braids.

The clothes Dorcas wore were dictated by her figure and she had learned that frilly, pretty clothes were unbecoming to her. For formal occasions Vernon had paid for two evening frocks to be made by a dressmaker in Exeter and these suited her admirably. One was in taffeta, of a green so dark that it was only when Dorcas moved that colour seemed to flow and merge like a river seen in shadow. The other dress was red – not scarlet nor poppy or flame, but the deep red of a good ruby – a colour so unsuitable for a young girl that Alma had made a faint protest. Dorcas refused even to consider another colour and Vernon had taken her side, baffled but amused by Dorcas's description of the shade as a *vindictive scribble of red*. She had been reading Browning at the time. It was when Lally and Dorcas were together the contrast in their styles was most apparent, Lally appearing frailer and more delicate than ever beside Dorcas, so large and so striking.

Over the last year Lally had gradually assumed her mother's position as consort to Billy Bassett and Coral lay on the day bed, Effie and a box of Milk Tray always to hand, while Lally, dressed in whatever Coral had chosen for her, sat through dinners and speeches of unimaginable boredom. She danced with men older than her father, always presenting a face so sweetly shy that no-one, not a single whisky-breathed, sweaty-handed one of them, ever guessed what went on in her head.

As Lally waltzed or quickstepped around the ball-room, competent from the dancing lessons that Coral had insisted she undergo, she saw, not middle-aged men, well-intentioned but maladroit, in dinner jackets stretched over sagging waistlines, nor bald heads sweating under the heat of the lights. What Lally saw were bodies lying tangled and distorted, the same bald heads detached from the same stringy necks; feet that had trodden on hers now mislaid, flesh and bone jagged and repulsive where they lay, disjointed, on the floor.

Coral was always waiting up when Lally arrived home, to take the exhausted girl through the whole evening for a second time. Lally had to relive for her mother every word she had spoken, every partner who had claimed her, the name of every woman to whom Billy had paid attention. Effie would wait until Coral flagged a little and then present Lally with a mug of Horlicks, urging her towards bed, tucking her in, stepping carefully around the splintered bones and slivers of flesh that encircled Lally's bed, cautious not to slip on the blood where it glowed in dark pools on the floor. When Lally awoke her room was as it had always been, pale and pretty, her dress of the night before suspended from a hanger on the back of the door where Effie had hung it, no sign at all remaining of the previous night's offensive.

Lally always slept in after a Saturday evening out with her father. This made her too late to go to her usual Mass at ten o'clock so that she had to attend High Mass at eleven and that meant fasting until almost midday. She became self-conscious about her breath, sure that it must smell, and she cleaned her teeth with great zeal, careful not to swallow even the water on her toothbrush which would break her fast and exclude her from taking Communion.

Lally had discussed this point in general with Mother Immaculata who had told her that she was allowing scruples to cloud her judgement but Lally knew that Mother Immaculata was wrong and that she must be on her guard and not allow any diminution in her obedience to the word of the Church. Once or twice Lally had become very faint but had always made it home in time, concealing from everyone but Effie how sick she felt. Effie would give Lally a glass of milk and dish up the meat and Yorkshire pudding as quickly as she could. She knew better than to suggest that Lally might forego Communion on those occasions.

It was when Lally was seventeen that Billy Bassett had made the decision that she was old enough to accompany him to the Bank's annual Dinner and Dance. Perhaps he imagined that Lally's involvement would encourage Coral to take a belated interest in his career; that a latent headache would remain undeveloped and that he would appear at one gathering at least with his wife at his side.

It was in the spirit of preparing a substitute to sit on the coach's bench that Billy suggested to Lally that she find a suitable frock and discuss with her mother the possibility of having her hair done for the occasion. If he had hoped by this ruse to change Coral's decision not to attend, he was disappointed. Coral took an almost vivacious interest in her daughter's launch on Penalverne society while remaining committed to her own dereliction of duty and seeming to be unmoved by Lally's obvious and growing distress.

On the day of the Dinner, Lally came down the staircase of the house in Advent Gardens dressed in so pale a pink that colour could hardly be discerned at all but as she walked paillettes concealed by layers of tulle gave a faint iridescence to her movements. Lally's wilful, almost white hair, stood out around her head like spun glass, small pink rosebuds confining some of its mass in a ribbon tied at the base of her neck.

Billy, who had been filling his hip flask for the rigours ahead, came out of the dining room in time to see his daughter's descent. He was caught by such conflicting emotions that the spontaneity of parenthood was diminished forever. It was as if the fairy from the top of the Christmas tree had been transposed to the good Wilton carpet of his house, delicate and too brittle to handle in the ordinary way. Billy had bought Lally a shoulder cape of white rabbit fur and now, confused and alarmed at his feelings, he fetched it from the front hall and placed it around her shoulders, trying not to be moved by the smell of baby powder with which Lally had dusted herself after her bath.

A taxi had been hired for the evening and Billy sat stiffly in one corner while Lally occupied the other, no emotion betraying that uppermost in her mind was the problem of how to conceal her feet.

Coral had chosen the material for Lally's dress and

had supervised her own dressmaker at each fitting. She had decided on pink roses and ribbons to tame Lally's hair, if that were at all possible, and had booked a shampoo and set for her at Maison Janette, a salon patronised by Coral herself and most of her middle-aged friends. She lent her daughter a tiny silver bag which was unwrapped from yellowing tissue paper, Coral coughing as a layer of dust danced in the light of her bedside lamp. Lally had asked about shoes.

'I've only got my summer sandals and they're not really suitable are they? Shall we go to Truro together to look for some evening shoes? I'd quite like silver, absolutely plain, with tiny heels.'

Coral had smiled and produced from the back of her wardrobe a pair of evening sandals, old and tarnished and rubbed where the buckle abraded the ankle strap. They were made of a silvered material, draped in a fold across the toe and poised on an ungainly heel.

Lally had started to laugh, thinking it a joke, but Coral had insisted, with a change of mood that alarmed her daughter, that the terrible shoes were what Lally would wear. 'They're silver and they fit you – what a good thing you've got such big feet for your age – and I don't want to hear any more about it. You've got the dress you wanted and there's nothing wrong with the shoes. They did me very well.'

Lally's unusual appeal overrode any of Coral's attempts to diminish her: the garish, shining earrings Coral produced from a jewel case were abandoned when, for her seventeenth birthday, Billy gave his daughter clips of aquamarine set in silver which matched the ring that came with them and which Lally wore on her right hand for the rest of her life. The stones reflected and enhanced the colour of Lally's unusual eyes as Billy had known they would, and with the string of pearls which came from her grandmother, Coral's influence retreated a little further. It was not defeated but waiting, armed and watchful, unwilling to relinquish any part of the investment she had made in her daughter.

Lally's evening dresses continued to excite comment wherever she went. They were like a box of fondant creams but when she removed the sugar-pink confection, or the violet or the mint green, she seemed to diminish. As each flower and bow was removed from her hair she saw herself declining, contracting into a pale reflection of herself, without substance or colour. Lally, dependent on her parents for money, accepted what was provided for her, tried to be grateful, and longed for some definition of who she was.

It was not until her grandmother died that Lally became hesitantly aware of her real potential but with this knowledge also came the burden of having to avoid any additional occasions of sin. For Judith Bassett's funeral Coral had pressed on Lally an old black dress of her own: it had a square, unbecoming neckline and faded patches under the arms and Lally, overwhelmed by its shabbiness, had said she would prefer not to wear black at all. Coral was unsure enough of her position with the Bassetts to be worried that she might be seen as the perpetrator of disrespect and agreed that Lally would have to buy a dress and together they went into town. Teresa Driscoll, working part time in the Ladies Department of Berrymans, took one look at the girl and produced perhaps the first garment Lally had ever had chosen for her that was suitable for her age. It was almost straight, just a slight flare to the skirt, unwaisted and styled like a sophisticated gymslip. Lally wore it over the white polo-necked jersey suggested by Teresa. who also slipped a pair of opaque black stockings into the carrier bag, smiling at Lally like a conspirator as she did so.

When Lally tried on this outfit, standing in front of the long cheval glass in her bedroom, what she saw emerging bewildered her. Gone was the uninviting image of a pale-faced girl in clothes so inappropriate as to be almost irrational. She saw instead the definition that she had so long desired; a young woman of original and unusual beauty, with hair like candyfloss and eyes that reflected the light around her, although their extraordinary translucence still overlaid unresolved apprehension and reserve.

Judith Bassett had left each of her grandchildren a small legacy and gradually the putty and sand of the clothes that Coral had chosen for Lally as being 'her' colours were replaced. While Lally's contemporaries wore skirts splayed out with many petticoats, and tight, bright, little tops and neck scarves, she stuck to black. Straight black dresses; tight black trousers that finished above her delicate ankle bones and which she wore with flat black ballet shoes. Her hair was confined by an Alice band, which was all she felt she wanted to do to subdue it as the contrast between the sobriety of what she now wore and the intransigence of her hair was part of the attraction which Lally was now beginning to understand she possessed.

Lally chose her new clothes with care; taste and style hardly more significant than modesty. If she wore a sleeveless dress in the house she would cover her arms with a bolero before going outside, or she would tuck a lace handkerchief into what, in someone more buxom, would have been described as her cleavage. Her excellent, if somewhat spare, figure she accepted as an affliction, a stumbling block of temptation in the path of others. Mother Mary John had said she was a vessel of purity which must not be defiled but, at seventeen, Lally had only an obscure acknowledgement of what that defilement might be. She took every care, nevertheless, to guard against it in case it stole upon her unawares and sullied her for ever.

Lally worked conscientiously. She noticed where help was needed in clearing dishes, in keeping the zinc and enamel surfaces of the kitchen clean and free from spills, and when she would be better employed in arranging extra plates of food. Her vigilance ensured that everything looked neat and professional as the afternoon wore on and the other young girls employed by Alma might have been tempted to allow standards to slip. Lally didn't join in the general chatter of the kitchen and after a while the other girls stopped trying to include her in their conversation, making faces behind her back or holding a finger under their nose in a gesture of perceived superiority.

Every time the double doors swung open Lally tried to establish from the corner of her eye that Eugene Jarvie wasn't standing there, tall and sleepy eyed, intent on disturbing her carefully ordered composure. Lally knew that it was unlikely that he would come into the kitchen at all and certainly not until the wedding was over and the bride and groom had left on their honeymoon. The rumour in the kitchen was that they were going to Italy after a night spent in Plymouth but Lally closed her ears to the speculation as to how the rest of the honeymoon would be spent.

As the kitchen doors opened and closed small sounds intruded; laughter, the tinkle of knives and forks on china. Once there was a crash, followed by silence and then more and louder laughter. Gerry had appeared, unabashed, with shards of glass piled on her tray, marooned in sticky puddles of wine. Lally had taken the tray from Gerry without a word and gone to find an Elastoplast for the finger that was leaking blood as red as the wine.

When Gerry had gone back to the reception Lally threw the broken glass into a box placed out of everyone's way in a corner near the room which Alma used as an office and which opened off the main kitchen. Long ago it had been a pantry but now it was enclosed and private. Wood panels were surmounted by glass and here Alma kept the accounts and order books, lists of staff and shift rotas, salesmen's cards and the names of emergency laundries and reliable plumbers. As Lally paused by the door she heard the telephone ringing in the office and looked around to alert Alma. Neither she nor Vernon was in the kitchen so Lally opened the door and picked up the telephone.

It was very dim in the little room and it seemed to smell of cigarettes and everything that had ever been cooked in the kitchen; fish and cabbage and stew, bread and burned jam. Alma's fountain pen was in a tray on her desk together with a silver propelling pencil, and there were several empty Gold Flake and Players packets. Lally counted five match boxes and opened one, finding, as she had expected, dead matches jumbled up with those still unused. It was one of the few habits which caused Vernon to raise his voice and for their first Christmas together he had given Alma an engraved silver lighter in an attempt to break her of this custom which annoyed him so disproportionately.

Lally's eyes strayed around the desk. Little piles of money; wild flowers in a mug, dying and scattering dry, curled petals on the papers around them; two photographs, one of Alma and Vernon's wedding, the other of Dorcas with her first pony. Lally looked again at the propelling pencil but her eye was distracted by a pottery cat, no bigger than a walnut and half hidden by a pile of dog-eared bus timetables. Her hand closed over it and she just had time to slip it into her pocket before Alma pushed open the door and came into the room.

'Did I hear the phone ringing just now?'

Lally nodded. *She didn't see, she couldn't have. And why shouldn't I? I've worked harder than anyone all afternoon but it's the others who've had all the fun.* 'It was Miss Westley.'

'Miss Westley?' For a minute Alma couldn't think of a Miss Westley. 'Oh! Do you mean Dorcas's aunt? That Miss Westley?'

'That's right, Aunt Alma, and I'm afraid that she had bad news. Dorcas's grandmother died this morning. She thought you ought to know.'

'Of course. Thank you, Lally.' Alma was looking at the desk and Lally kept very still. At last Alma said, 'I don't think we'll say anything to Dorcas until later on. There's no point in telling her now, we can't go down to Penalverne until Myrtle or Minnie tells us when the funeral is so Dorcas might as well enjoy the rest of the day. Lally?' Lally waited. 'You can never guess with Dorcas how she'll take things so I'll tell her myself later on and you won't say anything will you?'

'Of course not, Aunt Alma.'

'And, Lally, thank you for all you've done this afternoon, it's such a relief to know there's someone so reliable in the kitchen when I'm not there.' Alma patted Lally's arm. 'Back to the fray.' She smiled and

Lally watched her walk towards the swing doors, eyes noticing everything as she passed.

Lally started to say a prayer for the repose of Hetty Westley's soul, fingers clasped until they hurt around the pottery cat.

CHAPTER SIX

If Hetty Westley had died in the winter perhaps her funeral would have seemed more conclusive than it did. As it was Dorcas stood beside the mound of earth covered by artificial grass and thought how much it reminded her of the greengrocer's empty window. A memory had come quite suddenly to Dorcas from the time she had lived in Penalverne, that on half-day closing and on Sundays Mr Jelbart had arranged grass just like this, disguising the balding cloth and anchoring it down with bunches of artificial grapes and a few autumn leaves made of waxed paper secured to wire stems.

There were no grapes of course for Hetty, but a few wreaths, a very few, and even the sight of rosebuds and lilies with stiff white cards attached to them – *To Dearest Mother from Myrtle, Minnie and the late Roy, Mrs Westley with deepest sympathy from all at Penmere Road Chapel, From Alma and Dorcas in remembrance* – did little to distract Dorcas from a feeling of excitement which she knew to be inappropriate, but which even the presence of her two unfamiliar aunts failed to subdue. Dorcas tried to concentrate on the brass plate screwed centrally to the coffin lid. HENRIETTA DORCAS WESTLEY 1874–1952 it said but the words that Minnie Westley had whispered while they waited for the hearse to stop at the house still sounded loud in Dorcas's ears, louder than those being spoken to the handful of mourners who stood in warm sunshine around the grave of a woman whom hardly anyone would miss and still fewer mourn.

A light breeze which smelled of gorse teased Dorcas's skirt around her legs and in the distance she could see a woman with two small children weeding the rectangle of a family plot. There were flowers in a jar in the middle of the scattering of green chips which were spread over the top of the grave, and the grass surrounding it was trim and tidy. As Dorcas watched, one of the children stumbled and hit his head on the stone which surrounded this cared-for plot and he started to cry. His mother gathered him into her arms, kissing the hurt away, distracting him with one of her gardening tools, a fork or a trowel with a bright red handle. Dorcas was diverted from this picture by a butterfly of so bright a blue that it seemed to be made of the sky as it fluttered and winged its way around the flowers piled neatly beside the awful artificial grass.

Alma nudged Dorcas gently with her elbow as the undertaker's men allowed the straps threaded through the handles of the coffin to slip through their hands and her grandmother's earthly remains disappeared from sight. Dorcas thought of her father, and Myrtle Westley, covertly watching Roy's daughter, mistook the focus of Dorcas's grief, ready to blame Alma for the distance which had been allowed to grow between them. There was, Myrtle thought, no doubt that Dorcas was a Westley and Alma, aware of Myrtle's scrutiny, wished that Dorcas didn't favour quite so much the two dark, heavy women who stood on the other side of the hole in the ground.

As the small group walked towards their hired car the woman with the two small children came along the path under the yew trees. 'I was sorry to hear about your mother, Minnie, Myrtle. I hope Bobby didn't disturb you but I didn't realise the funeral was today and we've just been tidying up a bit. I like to do it every few weeks – can't have Dad in an untidy plot, you know how proud he was of his garden.'

'Thank you, Gaye. It was all very sudden, of course, but better for mother that she didn't linger.'

'Take a bit of getting used to though, you all being so close.' Gaye Odgers' eyes travelled to Dorcas. 'I can see who you are all right. You must be Roy's girl – just like your dad you are. Hello, Alma, remember me?'

'Of course I remember you, Gaye.' Alma smiled at the younger woman. 'You've got two lovely children.'

'Not bad are they? Considering.'

Dorcas wanted to ask what there was to consider

but Myrtle Westley took her arm and pulled her quite roughly towards the door of the car. 'Nice to see you, Gaye, but hardly the time or place for a chat. Goodbye now.' Myrtle's smile exonerated all and none of them as the big black car slid silently from the shade of the trees into the sunshine of the day.

Gaye watched it go. 'Bitch,' she said.

'What's bitch Mummy?' Bobby tugged at his mother's skirt. 'Mummy, what's bitch?'

'What?' Gaye looked at her son's upturned face. 'Bitch? No, lovey, I said *beach* – we'll go to the *beach* drec'ly. Would you like that? Come on, Bobs, get Gavin and we'll go home and fetch our swimmers.' Gaye watched the car carrying her cousin and her aunts until it turned through the gates, aware at the same time of the splattering of dry earth being shovelled on to the coffin. She knew that nothing would change even though Hetty was dead, Myrtle would see to that.

Minnie Westley removed damp tea towels from the plates of sandwiches that she and Myrtle had made that morning and covered with cloths to keep them fresh. She had removed the jam sponge from its greaseproof paper and taken fingers of saffron cake from the tin with some misgiving as to the suitability of eating cake which her mother had placed in the oven, leaving it to cook while she herself had sat down and died. Myrtle had told her sharply not to be sentimental and Minnie had hesitated, then, resigned to her sister's good sense, she had cut it into rectangles like a wedding cake and had placed the slices on a doily, radiating like the petals of some irregular golden flower.

'Can I give you a hand, Aunt Minnie?' Dorcas came into the kitchen carrying a glass of sweet sherry. 'Aunt Myrtle thought you'd better have this.'

'Oh my dear life, Dorcas, I had a sherry before we went to chapel and now another one! We only take a drink medicinally, you know, but I do believe that it makes me feel stronger.' Minnie took the drink in one swallow as if she had indeed been taking some unpalatable medicine but she smiled at Dorcas. 'I believe I could do with more medicine like that.'

'Shall I fetch . . . ?'

'. . . No, no dear, what would the others think?'

'My mother wouldn't think anything but I suppose you mean Granny's friends in the other room?' Mrs Daniels and Miss Treneer were representing the ladies of the chapel's Wednesday Club and every detail would be relayed to those unable to attend: the lightness of the sponge, the amount of seasoning in the egg sandwiches, the strength of the tea. Oh, and the medicinal sherry. Certainly the sherry.

'I'll make the tea if you like and you can go and talk to the others.' Dorcas noticed how her aunt's hands shook and the flush on her cheeks and she wondered at the strength of Minnie's medicine. 'Two teaspoons?'

'*Four*, dear, and plenty of hot water to top it up. I'll

take the sandwiches through with me and perhaps you'll bring the cake?' Minnie turned carefully, forgetting for a moment where her feet were. Dorcas put hot water in the teapot to warm it, opened the kitchen door and allowed her aunt to precede her down the dark little passage to the front room. Dorcas saw her mother glance at Minnie and hurriedly take the plate of ham sandwiches from her, grasping her elbow before removing the egg and cress bridge rolls from the other hand, all without looking at Myrtle or ceasing to speak to Dolly Treneer who had, long ago, tried to teach Alma and Coral the intricacies of maypole dancing when they were both too old for it and wholly disinterested.

Dorcas went back to the kitchen and scooped four spoonfuls of tea into the best china pot. As she waited for the refilled kettle to boil and for the tea to brew she looked around her. The walls were just as she remembered them, painted the colour of pea soup and supporting shelves on which were ranged enamel saucepans and a double boiler. There were canisters of yellow-and-white pottery, each with a label, *Flour, Rice, Porage Oats, Raisins, Bi-carb*. She recognised her grandmother's handwriting and, for the first time since she had heard of her death, Dorcas felt something other than a passing regret.

Dorcas opened a cupboard to replace the tea and was taken aback to see that it contained so little. There was a tin of cocoa, a pot of home-made jam and one of marmalade, sugar lumps in a cracked blue bowl and a bottle of coffee essence. Curious, she opened the drawer in the enamel topped table and saw that it held four knives, forks and spoons. There were, too, a very few utensils: knives whose broken blades had been rounded and smoothed to make them useful once more, spoons worn down to a razor edge. Dorcas could see nothing that was superfluous to the running of a thrifty household, no evidence of prodigality, no extravagance and very little of comfort. Old envelopes and scraps of paper were held together by a bulldog clip and hung from a nail next to a three-inch stub of pencil. The only real colour in the kitchen came from a calendar on the wall. It was a scene of rural implausibility made with scraps of metallic paper, the gold and pink and green catching the light and creating a small island of brightness in the otherwise cheerless room. Dorcas turned over the calendar and written on the back were the words, *Mother, Christmas* 1951, *affectionately Minnie.*

Dorcas put the teapot and water-jug on a tray covered by a cloth on which an embroidered crinolined lady edged sideways through a grove of hollyhocks, her bonnet supporting long ribbons which swirled and tangled with the flowers. Dorcas carried the tray to the kitchen door and then found she had no hand free to turn the handle so she had to go back to the table. She was spared the trouble of wedging open the door by Alma coming through it. There was an expression on Alma's face that Dorcas knew well, occasioned by many of the visitors to Petty Place:

it was amusement that needed to be suppressed by the demands of politeness.

'Minnie's absolutely blotto,' she said. 'Is there any hot water left?' Dorcas lifted the hinged lid on the water-jug. 'Do you suppose there's any coffee?'

'There's a bottle of Bev in the cupboard.'

'Well, that's better than nothing, I suppose. I'd better make her a strong cup. How on *earth* she got into that state, I can't imagine.'

'Medicinal sherries.'

'What?' Alma poured hot water into the cup.

'Aunt Minnie said that she and Aunt Myrtle only drink sherry medicinally so I suppose the medicine went to her head.'

'Unfortunately it went to her legs and those two old biddies in there are taking it all in – by tomorrow everyone in the chapel will know that Min was falling-over drunk.'

'Good job it was sherry then and not Cheltenham waters.'

'What are you talking about *now*?' Alma had spent too long with Roy's sisters and was exasperated.

> '"Here I lie and my four daughters,
> Killed by drinking Cheltenham waters.
> Had we but stick to Epsom salts,
> We wouldn't have been in these here vaults."'

'For goodness sake, Dorcas! Instead of quoting bad

poetry at me come and help me with your aunt. We'll have to pretend she's ill or overcome by grief or something.'

'Hold the door open then,' said Dorcas, as she picked up the tray again. 'Mum, Aunt Minnie whispered to me that Granny's left me this house. Do you think that can be true?'

Alma looked at her daughter, a younger, blither version of her aunts, and nodded her head. 'They want to tell you officially in a little while so I'm trying to get Minnie sober for the grand announcement.'

Mrs Daniels and Miss Treneer looked up as the door to the front room opened, their heads moving in unison as if joined by an invisible thread. 'Oh, here it comes – the cup that cheers but not inebriates.' Dolly Treneer's voice wobbled as she said this and she looked as if she wished that she had never spoken. Dorcas felt sorry for her and handed her the first cup of tea, while Alma sat beside Minnie and tried to interest her in a slice of cake and the strong coffee she had brought.

The front room of the little house seemed to be filled by the six women as they balanced plates and embroidered napkins on their laps, cups of dark tea in imminent danger of being upset by anything other than the most careful of movements. Dorcas put her teacup on the table, smiling as she thought of Cheltenham and keeping a covert eye on her mother, whose strategy seemed to be working. Minnie appeared brighter, talking a little too animatedly perhaps, although to Dorcas it seemed less a conversation than a string of clichés which encircled the gathered mourners, each fingering a bead before passing it on to her neighbour.

Mrs Daniels and Dolly Treneer refused a third cup of tea and rose together to kiss the air near the cheek first of Myrtle, and then of Minnie, their faces bright with importance. They shook hands with Alma and smiled at Dorcas before moving off together, perfectly in step, back to the heart of Penalverne to be for a little while the centre of attention as they discussed Minnie's problem and how much Dorcas had grown to resemble her aunts.

Among the ladies of the Wednesday Club there was no evidence but much speculation as to how Hetty Westley would have left her money for there had always been conjecture that the way Hetty had lived, abstemious and sparing to a degree, was by conviction and not necessity and that the Westleys would one day surprise everyone. Dorcas, certainly, was more than surprised to hear that she was now the owner of her grandmother's house and one third of all Hetty's assets. The gossips, for once, had not been wrong.

'But, Aunt Myrtle, where will you and Aunt Minnie live? This house is your *home*.'

Myrtle looked at Dorcas in a way that made her feel uncomfortable. 'We don't *live* here, Dorcas, not in this house. We live next door, don't you remember?'

Dorcas shook her head. 'I always remember you

being here, so I suppose I never realised that there were two houses.'

Myrtle shot a look at Alma but changed her mind about saying anything and turned back to her niece. 'My mother wanted you to have your father's share of everything, Dorcas, and Minnie and I quite agreed with that. It's as it should be and if you want to sell the house that won't worry us either; you must do exactly what you want with what now belongs to you.'

If Alma felt any bitterness at the neglect she had endured after Roy died she tried to suppress it for Dorcas's sake as she heard her daughter say only, 'Thank you, Aunt Myrtle.' In her mind's eye Dorcas saw the pea-green kitchen and the worn rugs and remembered pillows that felt as if they had been stuffed with rubble. She could still recall the cold white bathroom and the smell of Palmolive soap and Germolene and face flannels too infrequently washed. She remembered, too, sliding on polished linoleum until she fell and hit her head on the metal tray in the hallstand where umbrellas were left to drip and which still held her grandfather's walking sticks. Aunt Myrtle had told her to stop being such a baby and that she had been served right, but Aunt Minnie had taken her into the kitchen and found her a cream cracker. The cream cracker had tasted of soap but Dorcas, grateful for the attention, ate what she could while Minnie watched and then hid the rest in the pocket of her cardigan.

'There's no hurry, Dorcas.' Myrtle was talking again.

'Minnie and I would like a while to sort through mother's things but before you go, perhaps you'd like to have a look around and choose what you'd like to keep for yourself.' Myrtle turned towards her erstwhile sister-in-law. 'We wondered, Alma, whether you'd like the lustres as we remembered how much you used to admire them.'

'That's very generous, Myrtle. I'd love them if you really don't want to keep them for yourselves. They *are* so pretty.' Alma looked at the pink-and-crystal lustres on the mantelpiece but could think of nothing more to say and took refuge in lifting the lid of the teapot. 'Would you like more tea? I can easily make some fresh.'

'I'll go, I'll go. You sit still, you're the guest.' Minnie got to her feet and moved swiftly towards the door picking up the teapot as she passed. When she had gone Myrtle, Alma and Dorcas sat in silence. The wallpaper in this room was beige, faded to a pinky cast and covered in brown rambler roses. It was, Alma thought, as ugly a paper as she had ever seen and contrasted in a peculiarly disagreeable way with the dark red carpet and the heavy, faded curtains.

The long afternoon was drawing to an end and shadows thrown by the leaves of a clematis outside the window shivered through the glass and pattered over the women sitting inside. The air in the room was very close and enclosed everything in a smell of dust and polish and soot, reminding Alma of how much she had always disliked this house. Dorcas, too, felt oppressed and each time that she had a thought which she wanted to share with her mother she found its utterance blocked by a restriction in her throat, a dryness in her mouth.

Into this silence there came the sound of a crash followed by laughter as disquieting as it was unexpected. Myrtle stood up without a word and walked out of the room. Alma looked at Dorcas. 'We'd better go, don't you think? I can't take much more of this even for the lustres. Minnie must have found the medicine and taken another dose.'

'We can't just walk out.'

'Well then, we'll pop our heads round the door and say goodbye. Anyway, I should think Myrtle'd be glad to see the back of us.'

In the kitchen Minnie sat surrounded by fragments of what had been her mother's best teapot, leaves and water encrusting wall and floor. Myrtle hurried towards Alma. 'I'll take her home and come back later to clear up. It was good of you to come, Alma, I know how busy you are. And dear Dorcas.' Dorcas was startled at the warmth of her aunt's embrace. 'Come back soon to see us and we'll go through things together.'

If Dorcas felt any regret at her grandmother's death it was temporarily overlaid by knowledge and excitement. 'I'd like to drive back past Advent Gardens,' she said to her mother and smiled to herself as she thought of Coral and Billy avoiding each other in the empty rooms of the house, unaware of her sudden promotion.

✳   ✳   ✳

'Was it awful? I remember my Grandmother Paice's funeral and how everyone seemed determined to be jolly afterwards and how I felt really sad but no-one would allow me to show it. Daddy's friends kept telling me to brace up and keep a stiff upper lip.' Lally sat on Dorcas's bed, under instructions from Coral to find out if it were true, as she had heard, that Dorcas had come into a useful amount of money. Lally was not disposed to do as her mother suggested and spoke only of forgiveness of sin and purgatory, neither concept of any interest to Dorcas. Lally had been staying at Petty Place when Hetty Westley had died and, out of politeness, she had been included in the invitation to the funeral. Equally out of politeness she had declined.

On the day of the funeral Vernon was occupied organising a late booking for a birthday party, something which Alma would have done had she been there, and Lally had seen him drive away soon after Dorcas and Alma had left for Penalverne. Lally intended to make profitable use of the hours until Vernon returned.

Slowly and carefully, replacing everything just as she found it, Lally had gone through Alma's dressing-table, wondering at the shabbiness of her underwear compared with Coral's neat piles of satin and lace cami-knickers and petticoats; the disorder of stockings unpaired, jumbled together in confusion; the clutter of scarves and handkerchiefs tossed together in a drawer with no attempt at order or separation. Lally opened a box, repelled by the pink rubber bulb and tubing it contained: although she was not altogether sure what it could be, she slipped the instruction booklet into her pocket to read later on.

Alma's jewel case proved to be a worthwhile diversion. There were a few pieces that Lally remembered from the Penalverne days, an old-fashioned watch, now with a broken strap, two or three bracelets. Lally was touched to see that Alma still had the brooch made from beech husks, painted and stuck together on a safety pin that Dorcas had made for her – the one that Lally had made for Coral at the same time had long ago been passed on to Effie. Over the years these sentimental trinkets had been augmented by other, more valuable, presents from Vernon. He was a generous man and had given Alma jewellery which he felt to be in keeping with her new status. There were necklaces of garnet and peridot and at least two very good brooches and several pairs of earrings. As Lally expected, the diamond solitaire which Alma always wore was missing and the pearl studs and choker which she had put on to lighten the effect of her black dress and jacket.

Lally was self-conscious about her feet, Coral having convinced her that they were grotesquely large, but now she was surprised to find that they were as small as Alma's although even narrower. The shoes in the bottom of the wardrobe fitted her well enough as she tried on suede and leather and canvas, beguiled almost to euphoria by a black patent leather pair with heels as high and sharp as a dagger. In these she posed as she had seen Gerry do, legs unshapely and too pale, but still exciting in the sinful stilettos. Lally was so engrossed that she almost missed the sound of the vacuum cleaner moving steadily along the corridor and, just in time, returned all the shoes to Alma's cupboard before the door to the bedroom opened and the cleaner came in.

Lally smiled vaguely at her. 'I was looking for aspirin. I've been lying down but my head's no better so I thought I really should take something for it.'

Cath Dunscombe looked at Lally with dislike. 'There's some in the bathroom next door.' She added under her breath, 'No need to come in here at all.' It was Cath who had been questioned when Vernon's cufflinks had disappeared and Cath, whose sharp eyes and unsentimental appraisal of this frequent visitor, knew a great deal about Lally.

'Thank you, Cath, I should have thought of that myself.' Cath turned on the vacuum cleaner again and swept as close to Lally's feet as she dared.

Her discovery by Cath had disconcerted Lally so she went into the bathroom in case the cleaner should be listening, opening and closing the cabinet door with more force than was necessary. Lally had planned to search thoroughly through Dorcas's things once she had finished in Alma's room but that would have to wait now that Cath was working upstairs. In the meantime she decided that she would go and see Eugene Jarvie. She couldn't, of course, go and see Eugene himself but it would be perfectly reasonable of her to want to spend time with Gerry as Dorcas was away and everyone else was busy.

Eugene was working on his car in a corner of the yard at the side of the house where it ceased to be a farmyard but was not yet quite part of the garden. He looked up as Lally got off her bicycle and propped it against a wall. 'Hello, Lally, did you want me?' He chose the words deliberately, enjoying the confusion that crossed the girl's face as she tried to find a meaning less obvious than the one he offered.

'N ... no, I wanted to see Gerry. Is she about?'

Eugene watched the colour rise and fall in Lally's face, intrigued by the way the blue veins showed like scribble marks under her skin and how her pale hair looked as if it might crackle like broken icicles under his touch. This odd little friend of Gerry's had always seemed to be afraid of him and, although he would never have admitted such a thing to himself, Lally made Eugene uncomfortably aware of how easy it would be to hurt her. 'Gerry's around somewhere, probably out with the horses. I should have a dekko.' Eugene wiped his hands on a rag. 'Everyone else at the funeral, are they?' He wished that Gerry would appear so that he could be freed from the obligation of politeness.

'Dorcas and Aunt Alma are and Vernon's gone into town to buy things for a birthday party tonight. I don't think he really wanted to go to Penalverne anyway and this booking was a good excuse not to.'

'So you're at a loose end?'

Lally blushed again. 'Not really. Well, a bit I suppose.'

Eugene nodded towards a pile of clean cloths. 'You could polish the old girl for me if you like. She only needs buffing up and if you start at the back I can go on working under the bonnet. Looking good, isn't she?'

'Oh, Eugene, she's looking lovely. You've worked so hard on her you can hardly believe it's the same car.' Lally put a hand on the graceful wheel arch that swept down to the running-board of Vernon's old Austin 10. She removed her hand quickly but a print remained, a small palm with narrow, graceful fingers, and she rubbed at it with a cloth taken from the pile on the wall.

Eugene had worked for Vernon for nine months, logging his hours conscientiously at weekends and on any evenings he could spare until he had earned enough to buy the Austin. Vernon had recently bought himself a shooting-brake to collect guests from the local railway junction but he was sentimental about the narrow-bodied little car and glad that someone he knew was going to take care of it.

In certain lights the insignia it had worn during the war still showed and Vernon had always liked this. He made little effort to remove the markings as they reminded him that the Austin had served the Royal Air Force as a staff car, driven in London during the Blitz and coming through almost unscathed. The car had survived, just as he had done, and now Vernon felt protective towards it, allowing the faint markings to remain, puzzled about the sweet, flowery smell that occasionally drifted through the interior, over the plump green leather seats, filling the car with secrets. Not everyone experienced this mystery: Dorcas never had and if Eugene had wondered about it, he certainly never spoke of it to anyone.

When Eugene had gone to Vernon with his proposition, Vernon readily agreed to sell the car, fairly certain that Eugene would not persevere in raising the money. Eugene, who worked outdoors and spent as little time as he could inside four walls, had tackled jobs that he detested throughout the summer and into the winter and Vernon saw that his assessment of the boy's determination had been mistaken. Now they had an understanding and Eugene tended the Austin with care, hiring it back to Vernon for wedding parties and photographs at Petty Place.

Lally worked painstakingly. Mindful of scratches she flicked away any dust before polishing each small area of black paintwork, wrapping the duster around every spoke in the wheels, rubbing carefully at the lights and the short rear bumper. When Lally reached the door handles she hesitated. To continue forward would be to draw very close to Eugene: she might even, inadvertently, touch him, feel the warmth of his body, catch the trace of his own particular smell. Lally concentrated on the running-board, using the dirtier of the dusters, seeing as she looked down, Eugene's feet in a pair of old tennis shoes with holes in the toes, one held together with string instead of a lace.

Lally walked around to the far side of the car and polished very slowly along the bonnet and over one of the big round headlights, and then stopped, hesitating, watching the back of Eugene's head bent inside the bonnet of the car so close to her that she could have stretched out a hand and laid it on his dirty blue shirt. His hair was almost as pale as hers but the hairs on his arms were thick and gold and disturbing. Lally moved and Eugene looked up as if he were surprised to see her still there.

'I've finished. All except the bit where you're working.'

'Thanks, Lally, that's great.' He glanced at the side of the car nearest to him and then back at Lally. She seemed to be waiting for something but he said again, 'Thanks a lot. I don't know where Gerry's got to – do you want to wait or shall I give her a message when I see her?'

'Oh, just say I came over. Here are the dusters.' Lally had folded the cloths into neat squares and as she handed them to Eugene his fingers touched hers and she drew her hand away as if it had been burned. Eugene watched thoughtfully as Lally walked to the bicycle propped against the wall. As she mounted and pedalled away she looked very small, about twelve years old, just as she had done when Eugene had first seen her. Dorcas and Gerry were young women now but Lally, at this distance, still looked like a child, vulnerable and unprepared.

When Lally left the farm she didn't return immediately to Petty Place but cycled on to the point where the lane met the main road and from where visitors had their initial view of the house. When Dorcas had been brought to Petty Place for the first time it was from here that she had looked across the landscape and believed it to be colonised by horses and where Alma was sure there had been an inland sea of bluebells. Lally laid the bicycle down in the long grass and sat beside it under an ash tree.

She was on the bank of a stream and there were two or three cows standing up to their hocks in the cool of the water. She knew enough now to recognise them as Devon Reds, big, gentle animals which made up half of Eugene's father's herd of milking cows. Beyond the stream in a sunlit field a baler was standing, abandoned in ribs of greyish hay and Lally wondered why it should be there. Perhaps one of Eugene's brothers, Aidan or Greg, had been called away to another job; perhaps Eugene himself should be baling in the field, not messing about with his car.

Lally closed her eyes and thought about Eugene and knew her thoughts to be impure. It worried her that she couldn't get to confession until she went back to Penalverne as she'd never again ask Aunt Alma to take her into the nearest Catholic church. It had caused such a commotion last time and in the end it was Vernon who had said that he would take Lally with him when he went to collect some guests from the station, but Lally had been late back to the arranged meeting-place and Vernon had gone without her. He had needed to make another journey to fetch her as it was beginning to rain with flat, heavy squalls that flooded the ground, leaving the air damp and thick until the sun burned through the clouds again.

Lally had waited until she was sure that Vernon had forgotten her and had then set off to walk the four miles back to Petty Place. She was soon soaked to the bone, her skirt stuck to her legs, clinging and uncomfortable, her hair dripping on to the shoulders of her cotton shirt. When Vernon found her, Lally was walking awkwardly, shuffling, trying to keep on a sandal whose strap had broken. They had driven home, Lally fearful that she was sinning again because of the anger she felt towards Vernon, and Vernon, for once, silent with reproach.

Lally sat in the shade of the trees and knew that she should banish Eugene from her thoughts and she started to pray for help. ... *that never was it known that anyone who fled to your protection, implored your help, or sought your intercession was left unaided. Inspired by this confidence, we fly unto you, O Eugene.* No, that wasn't right. Lally tried again ... *O Virgin of Virgins, our Mother.* That was better, that should silence the mocking voice in her head once and for all.

Lally tried to focus on the cows in the water, half in

and half out of the shadow, sunlight breaking through the new, late leaves of the ash tree to paint their red hides with pale patches. The elm trees at the far end of the field were in full leaf and buttercups shone silkily golden between them. Lally had brought Effie here, to this magic place, but Effie had seen only the ashes of a fire that picnickers had left behind, paper and bottles strewn among the bushes, and eggshells and orange peel gaudy on the summer grass. Together Effie and Lally had collected all the rubbish, carrying it home tied in Effie's scarf but Lally had never taken Effie back there and seldom spoke of it to anyone.

Now, as she sat on the grass listening to birds calling in the trees and watching the tiny movements of insects in the frothing heads of cow parsley, Lally thought only of Eugene: of the way the sun shone through his over-large ears, illuminating them to a transparent tender pink, and of his eyes which she was afraid to meet. *A man can tell immediately what you think of him if he looks in your eyes. You must guard your eyes at all times.* Mother Mary John's words which brought apprehension to Lally. Did Eugene, she wondered uneasily, know how she felt about him? She had looked in his eyes once or twice and had seen nothing but puzzlement, but he must know. Why couldn't she tease him and treat him as naturally as Dorcas did, talking to him as easily as she did to Gerry and as she had once done to Lally herself?

But Lally was different, she knew that. She was special, hadn't Coral always said so? Didn't the nuns take extra care with her, reinforcing the high standards which Lally set for herself, helping in the only way they understood to strengthen her resolve to silence the inner voice which prompted her to such excess? Mother Scholastica had explained to Lally that the devil was trying hard to subsume her but that she could, she *would*, triumph over the forces of evil if she exerted enough will power.

Lally watched the cloud shadows on the fields and knew what she had to do about Eugene. She understood that she needed to be near him, to put her own redemption in jeopardy until such time as he was safe and she could relinquish her vigil.

Lally picked up the bicycle, finding a twig to knock off the slug that was crawling across the handlebars, disturbed from its exploration of the long, damp grass. As she cycled back to Petty Place the car bringing Dorcas and Alma home passed her and Lally waved, resolute in her new understanding, unaware that, as far as Dorcas was concerned, she was already rather too late.

'Well, *was* it awful?'

'Not if you compare it with my father's funeral. Actually it was a bit pathetic; there was hardly anyone there and even the minister couldn't come back to the house as he had an urgent visit to make. Just as well, really.'

'Why? What happened?

Dorcas kicked off her shoes. 'Aunt Minnie who, by the way, isn't half as bad as I'd remembered her, got tiddly and fell over and broke Granny's teapot. I say she *got* tiddly, but I think she was already tiddly before we arrived.'

'I thought the chapel people weren't supposed to drink.'

'They're not but Mum said that Aunt Min first started on the Wincarnis when she was run down after flu or something. Mum didn't seem at all surprised and she and Aunt Myrtle just carried on as if nothing had happened although I'm sure Granny's friends knew what was going on. They looked so *avid* somehow.'

'You are funny, Dorcas. *Avid* – for what?'

'I don't know. Excitement, perhaps; something different and scandalous to report back to the rest of the coven. You're the one who's supposed to know all about those sort of things, loving your neighbour, speaking no evil and all that. Anyway, that wasn't the most interesting thing that happened.' Dorcas looked sideways at Lally. She seemed calm, the discomposure which so often seemed to accompany Lally these days suspended, or at least overlaid with a temporary concern for Dorcas. 'Have you ever heard of someone called Gaye Odgers? About oh, thirty, two little boys?'

'I've heard the name.' Lally was cautious.

'Well they were in the cemetery and she came up to speak to us and Aunt Myrtle practically threw me into the car so I didn't get a chance to say anything.

Do you suppose she was a Pretender, come to claim the throne from the rightful heir?'

'You read too much rubbish, Dorcas. My mother says reading's just an escape to you, an excuse not to have to deal with the real world.'

'Well, she'd know all about that.'

'What do you mean?' Lally's hands, hidden in the folds of her skirt curled into fists. 'Just what do you mean by that, Dorcas?'

'Oh, just forget about it. I'm so tired that everything seems to be coming out muddled.' Dorcas threw herself backwards on to the bed. 'I didn't mean *anything*, Lally. Tell me what you did today.'

Lally could feel her heart beating. It seemed to be in her throat, on her tongue, a fibrillation that Dorcas intended to choke her. She swallowed and willed her thoughts away from danger. 'Actually,' Lally said, 'I spent ages with Eugene.' The words were out, she was safe again.

'Oh, did you?' Dorcas seemed to be amused. 'Did he make you clean that old heap of a car? That's what he usually does to the girls who follow him around.' Dorcas turned her head towards Lally. The room was halfway between light and dark, everything grey, soft and colourless. Dorcas was very tired: she knew she shouldn't have spoken unkindly to Lally about her mother but Lally was so passive, so uncomplaining, that sometimes Dorcas wanted to goad her, to awaken her to the knowledge that Coral was a fraud, an imposter, whose duplicity furled and encompassed the life of everyone in the house in Advent Gardens.

'Lally?' In the glass that stood on Dorcas's dressing-table she saw reflected the three faces of her friend. 'Oh, come on Lal, I don't seem to be able to say anything right tonight, do I? I didn't mean it about Eugene; I'm sure he was very glad of your help. What else did you do?'

'We talked.'

'And?'

'I went for a bike ride and made a big decision.' *Careful, careful, tell Dorcas only what she needs to know. Your secret sacrifice must be just that, a secret. Don't let Dorcas in on it so that she and Gerry can laugh and make fun of you.* 'I've decided not to go back to school in September and to do the secretarial course Mummy wants me to.'

'Are you sure, Lally? Really, really sure?' Dorcas, half asleep, pulled herself up on to her elbows. 'You've always worked so hard and you're the only one of us who could go on to university if you wanted: I'm much too thick and Gerry seems to have missed the boat rather. Just think about it a bit more — you don't *have* to do everything Aunt Coral says, you know. You are allowed to make up your own mind about things.'

'You don't understand, Dorcas. Mummy says that a secretarial training is something you can always fall back on and I don't want to upset her, especially now that she's got to have an operation. If I'm at home I'll be there to help her . . .'

'. . . That's what Effie's there for,' Dorcas inter-
rupted. 'Why do you insist on being such a martyr,
Lally? Effie'd be much better at looking after Aunt
Coral anyway.'

'I want to do it, truly I do. Mummy's never been
properly well since I was born and it's the least I can
do to make it up to her.'

'Well, I jolly well wouldn't, even if Alma wanted
me to, which she wouldn't in any case, but I'm going
to do exactly what I want whenever I find out what
it really is.' Dorcas closed her eyes and like a tired,
contented child, fell asleep almost immediately.

Lally looked at her friend, plain and determined
even in sleep, with an expression that hinted at secrets,
amusement hidden behind the flat planes of her face.
Lally wanted to hear what Dorcas thought she wanted
to do but sleep had intervened and now the opportunity
was lost. One thing Lally did know with certainty and
that was that whatever Dorcas decided on was the thing
that would come to pass. Lally felt a wave of guilt engulf
her, almost a physical weakness, as she tried to silence the
voice that told her that it was utter absurdity to believe
that the meek would inherit the earth: the earth would
go to whoever grabbed it and held on fast, and that
was something that she was learning to accept.

Lally thought about Gerry, knowing that Dorcas had
missed the point about her friend's reluctance to leave

home. Lally thought it unlikely but perhaps Dorcas didn't yet know that Gerry had been accepted at the art school and would start there in the autumn. 'I'm not much good at anything in particular,' Gerry had said to Lally, 'but I can draw a bit so I suppose I'd better give it a go and see what I *can* do.' She had laughed. 'Mother Scholastica always said she was wasting her time on me and I think she was probably quite right but I can always teach and then I'll have long holidays, which will suit me very well.' Gerry had been smoking as she said this, watching Lally with amusement as they sat on the wall at Home Farm encouraging Aidan and Greg, who were trying with little success to corner the boar. Lally had tried to conceal her distaste for Gerry's dirty bare feet and what she perceived as her immodesty in exposing a naked midriff between shorts and an old shirt of Eugene's which she had tied around her middle in an attempt to make it fit.

'Will you live at home?'

'Of course.' Gerry was suddenly serious. 'My mother needs help with the little ones and they're all terrified of me so they behave themselves when I'm around.'

'That's not true, Gerry, you're wonderful with them.' Lally stopped. 'Is that why you've stayed at home until now?' She was suddenly ashamed of her silent assumption that Gerry was lazy and self-indulgent and aware of the sacrifice it had been for the older girl to allow her talent to lie fallow. 'Isn't your mother any better then?'

'Mum's absolutely fine now but seven children do

make a lot of work and none of the girls she has to help her ever stay long. Can't face the Jarvies *en masse* it seems.' Gerry took another lungful of smoke. 'Little Bebe's starting at the kindergarten in September so Mum'll have some time to herself at last and if she's sensible there won't be any more babies.' Gerry looked sideways at Lally. 'Don't be shocked. It's just that you see things differently when you're the oldest of seven and you've nearly lost your mother having one baby too many. We all adore Bebe of course, but I can't agree with the Church's teaching any more and before you ask, yes, it does cause me great concern – just something I've got to work out for myself.'

'I'm sorry, Gerry.'

'Whatever for?' The boar had evaded the corrugated iron and yard brooms with which the boys had armed themselves and stood in the middle of the cobbles, saliva dripping from its tongue, little eyes mad with anger. 'What are you sorry for, Lally?'

'For misjudging you. You've got a huge talent and I hope you do really well at art school. You deserve to.'

Gerry threw the stub of her cigarette in an arc over the bushes behind them. 'Don't get all sincere with me, Lally, I'm not used to it.' She smiled at her friend. 'Eugene's got a rude name for friends like us – you know, people really close to you that you're quite comfortable with – and I like the way we've always pretended to annoy each other. I wouldn't want to change that, it makes life more fun.'

'But everything *is* changing. I suppose this is the last summer that we'll be able to do exactly what we like.'

'I shall always do what I like.'

'I don't expect that you will. Nobody can.'

'Wait and see.' Gerry swung herself down off the wall. 'Dorcas used one of her quotations to describe all of us once. *Eating Grapes Downwards* — do you know what she meant?

Lally shook her head. 'I often don't.' She smiled at Gerry. 'Do you? Honestly?'

'I do this time because she explained it to me. It means that someone like you, conscientious and scrupulous, eats the small, sour grapes first, moving up the bunch and promising yourself all the best ones as a treat in the end, while someone like Dorcas grabs and eats the plump, juicy one at the top of the bunch first.' Gerry looked at Lally before she went on. 'What it actually *means*, you see, is that by the time you've dutifully disposed of the nasties you may be too full to be able to enjoy the best grapes. Or that they've gone off by then, of course.'

'And Dorcas, eating downwards?'

Gerry laughed. 'Just the opposite. She's taken what she's wanted and can't be bothered with the things that aren't so nice — the sour, small grapes if you like — so she just leaves them or throws them away.'

'I see. I think I do, anyway. What about you, Gerry?'

'Haven't worked that out yet although Dorcas says

I start in the middle. Come on, let's go and find Eugene and make him take us out for a drive. We've earned it, all the hours we've spent cleaning and polishing his beastly car.'

'Oh no, you go Gerry. I promised Aunt Alma that I'd arrange the flowers for the tables tonight and I'd better go. Except that I'm scared to cross the yard because of that awful animal. Can't Greg and Aidan do anything with it?'

Gerry laughed. 'I'll race you across to the house and I'll tell Eugene that you were longing to come with me but that your sense of duty meant that you had to go and help with the flowers. He'll be heartbroken: can't imagine why but he really likes you, you know.' She lit another cigarette before turning to Lally and saying, 'Right? Ready, steady, go,' and flying on bare, vulnerable feet across the yard and into the safety of the back door of the house. Lally watched Gerry go, too afraid to follow where she led, conscious of a great happiness. Eugene liked her, that was all she needed to know, it was enough for now and more than she had dared to hope for. With a rattle of metal and a great surge of noise, Eugene's brothers closed in on the boar and drove it, screaming and slipping, back into its pen and Lally slid safely down the wall and went to fetch her bicycle.

Dorcas was deeply asleep when Lally stood up and

left the quiet bedroom. There was still time to ring her mother and say that she would be home at the weekend and that she would enrol at The Penalverne Commercial Academy for the autumn commencement. That way, Lally thought, at least I shall be where I'm needed when Mummy is recuperating and no-one will be able to say other than that I did what was expected of me. I did God's will.

CHAPTER SEVEN

'When you visit me tomorrow I want you to bring a shorthand notebook with you.' Coral was slumped against two pillows in the uncomfortable position of neither lying nor sitting. Her oyster satin nightdress was crumpled and her scalp was beginning to itch, her regular shampoo and set overdue. 'I want to write thank you letters to the wonderful friends who've sent all these cards. I would do it myself but there are so many of them and I'm not really up to it yet and I thought that as your shorthand's so good I could dictate a wee note to you and you could type it out for me.' Her voice was carrying, insinuating itself into every corner of the small ward, sneaking around the ramparts of *Woman's Weekly* and *Housewife* erected by Coral's fellow patients from behind the shelter of which they exchanged bemused glances as they waited for their own, less entertaining, visitors.

'My typing's not very fast yet but I could try. How many letters were you thinking of?'

Coral laid her hand on the pile of cards on her bedside table. 'Oh, at least twenty-five – probably more.' She knew quite well that there were exactly fourteen and picked one from the top of the pile as if at random. 'Did I show you this one from Lady Carclew?'

'Yes, yesterday.' Lally knew that Audrey Carclew's message would become a permanent fixture on Coral's mantelpiece just as the Christmas card from the Lord Lieutenant was placed each year in a position central to the seasonal display at the house in Advent Gardens. 'Have you heard from Dorcas and Aunt Alma?'

Coral riffled through the cards and slid one face down across the bed to Lally. 'It's what I should have expected I suppose – not even funny, just vulgar.'

'There's not much choice in the village shop up there. This was probably the best they had and at least they remembered you.'

'Always sticking up for them and I can't imagine why. Since,' Coral hesitated, aware of the listeners behind the blockade of borrowed magazines, 'well, ever since you-know-who arrived on the scene you've just been cast aside like an old shoe but you're so loyal, such a very faithful girlie that it doesn't make any difference to you, does it? I just hope that Dorcas appreciates how lucky she is, having you as her oldest friend.'

Lally looked at her mother. As she turned her head Lally became aware of deep puckers on Coral's upper lip, half hidden by a thicket of bleached, greyish hairs, and the way soft, blue skin formed pouches under her eyes; pouches that looked like blisters, inflated and fluid. As Coral moved stale air escaped from the bedclothes and Lally turned aside, disgust like a hand at her throat. 'I'll bring a notebook then,' she managed to say. 'Is there anything else you need?'

'Effie will be in tomorrow with some clean laundry but what I really need is to see my girl every day.'

'You know I'll be here as soon as I can and Daddy said that tomorrow he'll come in the afternoon because we're going to the cocktail party at the golf club in the evening.'

Coral didn't answer and tried to move herself up in the bed, sliding down again on the shiny incline of her nightdress. She was beginning to feel provoked by Lally's impassivity and wondered why her daughter had brought with her no more than a bunch of pinks and a holy picture. Lally had stood the little card of the Infant of Prague in his triangular dress on Coral's table and had found a vase for the flowers but Coral wanted more: she wanted chatter and laughter like the other women in their cheap cotton nightdresses looked forward to; black grapes and expensive blooms, too large and so inconvenient that they had to be moved at meal times. She was affronted by a small bunch of inconspicuous flowers, however sweet they smelled.

'I saw Mother Immaculata yesterday and she said to tell you that she's making a novena for you.'

'That should make *all* the difference. What does that old crow know about women's problems or the way we suffer for bringing children into the world.'

'I didn't think your gall bladder was part of the process of reproduction.'

'It saddens me to say this, Mary Marigold, but you've become very hard lately; almost uncaring, just like your father, and if you can't appreciate all that I'm going through perhaps it would be better if you stayed away for a while.'

'What about the letter you want to dictate? If I stay away you won't be able to will you?'

Dear Lady Carclew, Your card is expensive but tasteless and the sentiments you express are exactly those you would send to any member of the Union of Catholic Mothers. My gall bladder had become diseased not, as you may think, by the injudicious consumption over many years of fried foods and cream cakes, but by the conception and gestation of a child who has now turned her face away from me and who thinks more of Mother Immaculata than she does of her own mother. You may be surprised to hear that this same daughter, Mary Marigold Bassett, is in love with Eugene Jarvie and it is for this reason and this alone that she spends so much of her time away from Penalverne and in the company of Dorcas Westley, a girl who has no appreciation of the subtleties of normal trust and honesty, qualities to which Mary Marigold holds fast with all the tenacity of a true child of the Church.

The voice in her head dictating to Lally faltered, not sure how to end such a letter: *Best wishes, Yours sincerely* — or perhaps something more familiar. The words she heard had been quite distinct and Lally was almost surprised that Coral didn't supply the answer she sought. She waited for her mother to speak.

'Of course I don't really want you to stay away. I didn't mean anything by what I said – it's just that I'm feeling so peaky.' Coral managed a few tears and Lally found her a handkerchief and watched as her mother carefully dabbed at the new soft skin under her eyes. 'I do so look forward to seeing you but my bottie's so sore, sitting here all the time, and I'm so *hungry*.'

'Once you're home again Effie can build you up with pies and milk puddings and all the things you like.'

Coral's mouth drooped. 'I never realised that the food in here would be quite inedible, and the nurses check my locker every day you know. I don't know what they expect to find in there but they don't seem to be averse to eating my choccies and saying it's for my own good.'

'Well, Daddy did offer to pay for a private room.'

'And then I'd never have seen anyone and just had to lie there on my own for hours and hours.'

'Cheer up, Mummy, you'll be home soon and I'm praying for you as hard as I can ...'

'... Oh do stop, Lally, you make me tired.' Lally stood up to leave but Coral hadn't finished. As the girl walked towards the door Coral called after her, 'I hadn't forgotten the cocktail party you know. You will drop in to let me see you in your frock won't you? I want you to wear the dusky rose and tell Effie to make sure that it's properly pressed this time.'

Lally hesitated. 'Not the rose.'

'Why ever not? It suits you so well.'

'I haven't got it any more and, besides, I've bought myself a dress I like much better.'

'Come back here this minute, Lally, and tell me what you're talking about. What do you mean that you haven't got the rose dress? What have you done with it?'

'I gave it to Mother Mary John.' Lally was quite calm, knowing herself to be protected from the wilder extravagances of her mother's pique by the public nature of their conversation. 'She said that they were starting work on the costumes for the nativity play and she wondered if we had any old material we could spare that they could use for the robes for the three kings. Apparently the shepherds' things are easy but the kings needed something more sumptuous than the collecting boxes turned up and I thought of my dress and how much material there was in the skirt, so I gave it to her.'

'Well you'll just have to ask her to give it back. Have you any *idea* how much that dress cost? Whatever were you thinking of, you silly girl?'

The small ward was very quiet. Only a couple of visitors remained and Coral became aware of their unconcealed interest. Her voice dropped. 'What about the dress you've bought? I expect it's totally unsuitable and how could you afford it?'

'Daddy gave me some money and it *is* suitable: it suits me much better than the pink ever did.'

'I should have guessed; he can't deny you anything, and where did you get it? Berrymans? That might not be too bad as at least they know what I like and could probably be relied on not to let you make a fool of yourself.'

'No, not Berrymans.' Miss Hawkey and Mrs Spargo waited and heard Lally say, 'As a matter of fact I saw it in the window of The Bandbox and it was just the kind of thing I've always wanted, so I went in on Friday afternoon to try it on.'

'*The Bandbox!* And on Friday when I was here, alone, under the knife.'

'Be fair, Mummy, there wasn't anything Daddy or I could do for you at the time was there? And we were both here when you came round, waiting to see how you were. Now, about coming in tomorrow,' Lally persisted, emboldened by the presence of strangers, 'if we do, we'll be late picking up Daddy's friends and he ought to be at the club when the party starts as he is one of the hosts. It wouldn't be very convenient really, to come here first, I mean.'

Little rivulets of sweat trickled down Coral's temples. She wanted to reach out across the distance from her bed to where Lally was standing and if Lally were untouchable in her implacable righteousness then Effie would have to do, but Effie wasn't here either. She was at the house in Advent Gardens sliding a cottage pie into the oven to warm through for dinner and opening a tin of marrowfat peas which she knew were a favourite with Billy but which Coral refused to serve, too acute a reminder of all that she had left behind.

'What friends of Daddy's? I didn't know you were taking anyone else with you.' Lally began once more the slow glissade towards the door. 'Come here, Lally, and tell me what friends.'

'Someone called Davy Hosegood who lives at the top of Paul Hill.'

'You said "friends". Who else?'

'Teresa Driscoll.'

'You mean this Davy Hosegood is taking that Driscoll woman to the party?'

'I suppose so. I don't really know, I didn't ask. I just know that his car is being resprayed so Daddy offered to collect him and Teresa so, you see, we really shouldn't be late.'

'They'll just have to wait if your father's busy and I've never heard him mention a Davy Hosegood.'

'Please, Mummy, don't spoil the evening for him.' Coral was gratified to hear the pleading note in Lally's voice. Just a little more pressure and Coral knew that Lally would capitulate.

Coral appeared to be thinking over what Lally had said. 'Well, I suppose it wouldn't look good if your father isn't there to welcome the guests even though they all know how ill I've been. What we'll do is compromise: you wear your new dress when you come in after class tomorrow so that I can see for myself how you look and we'll forget about you both visiting in the evening. I'll tell Effie to come in instead.'

'I think Effie's going out and what about the letter you want me to take down for you?'

'The letter can wait one more day and Effie won't mind,' Coral half smiled. 'Now come and give me a kiss before you go. I can see you're longing to run away.' As Lally leaned over her mother she felt sharp fingers digging into the soft flesh at the top of her arms and rejoiced at the thought of her rose pink dress, and the ankle length sea-green skirt, even now being stitched into little tunics and cloaks by Mother Mary John's grateful hands.

I do love my mother: I do, I really do and I want her to get better very soon. I don't know what I'll do if she dies because it's all my fault that she's ill. If she hadn't had me she wouldn't be ill all the time and she wouldn't have needed this operation and all I do is annoy her and that doesn't help her at all. Please, please make her better soon because I do love her. Lally hardly thought anymore of the words she was saying to herself. The burning centre of her consciousness knew them by heart: they accompanied her waking and her sleeping and had become a meaningless mantra that accompanied her wherever she went, whatever she did, a shield that stood between the truth and unacceptable reality.

When Lally got back to Advent Gardens the house was unusually quiet. Billy was not yet home and Effie had gone to the Savoy to see *High Noon*. It was her second visit of the week, the expense justified by the pleasure she gained by watching Gary Cooper, her favourite film star of the moment. In time the film's insistent theme tune would become part of her repertoire, bubbling and escaping in moments of excitement.

There was a note on the kitchen table reminding Lally that there was a pie in the oven and that the gas needed to be lit under the saucepan, but Lally wasn't hungry. She poured herself a glass of milk and walked around the empty kitchen while she drank it, opening cupboards and drawers at random. The kitchen had recently been painted and was now cream, red handles having been substituted for the previous green and new curtains hung at the window, stylised tomatoes and lettuce and radishes scattered at random alongside mushrooms and cauliflowers. Effie had hemmed offcuts of the curtain material into napkins, one of which she had placed beside the plate she had laid for Lally and another at Billy's place. Effie had also left a *crème caramel* on the table under a cover which she had crocheted, the edges of the material weighted down with coloured beads which hung in a frieze like cloudy jewels. Lally removed this, digging at the shiny, slippery surface of the pudding, eating two or three spoonfuls before pushing it aside.

What she wanted was chocolate: squares of Dairy Milk to coat her teeth and tongue, Fry's Chocolate Cream to stick to the roof of her mouth, and a bar of Five Boys to crush and squeeze into melting, liquid consolation. There would be chocolate in Coral's bedroom Lally was certain and she left the kitchen, which was as silent and clean as a convent, to look for what she knew would be out of sight in the bedside cabinet or hidden behind a pile of magazines on the window seat. Her parents had slept apart since Coral had found excuse enough to do so and as Lally passed her father's room, she smelled his familiar presence through the half-open door and lingered for a minute, aware of none of the pernicious culpability for Billy's unhappiness that lay so close to the surface of her feelings for her mother.

In Coral's room Lally stood still, looking around her as if for the first time. As in her own bedroom there was a crucifix over the bed but Coral's was of ivory, chased and carved and elaborate, a present from Judith Bassett at the time of Coral's reception into the Church. A pile of small prayer books, a Missal, a Garden of the Soul, lay on the shelf of the night table and a statue of St Antony stood on the windowsill. As she observed all this Lally wanted to pull down the crucifix; to tear page after page from the Missal beside her mother's bed. The Table of Moveable Feasts would go, the Mass of a Virgin not a Martyr, Palm Sunday. The Feast of Corpus Christi would follow Benediction and the Way of the Cross: Latin and English, red printing and black, all ripped, shredded, destroyed. St Antony with his overpainted, androgynous face would lie in fragments in the fireplace and all the transient, gaudy pretence of Coral's conversion would be despoiled, exposed for what it was, a convenience, a contrivance for her self-advancement and a medium for holding Lally in subjection for as long as Coral chose.

Lally felt St Antony's robes, stiff and cold under her fingers. She saw the smile on his face turned towards the Infant cradled in his arms before she opened her hand and watched the slivers and shards of pottery disintegrate into powder at her feet. Brown, yellow, white; a pink cheek, a baby's fat little hand, all fractured beyond repair.

Lally went downstairs to fetch the dustpan and brush and when she had wrapped the debris in three layers of newspaper so that no-one would cut their fingers on the sharp edges, she put it all into the dustbin and went into the kitchen to help herself to the food that Effie had left for her, rescuing the peas just as they began to catch on the bottom of the pan. Lally ate a large helping of cottage pie with another glass of milk and several coffee creams which she had liberated from the box which she had found hidden in her mother's stocking drawer.

As Lally was enjoying the last of the chocolates she heard the back door opening and caught the unmistakable sounds of Effie in a good mood. There was a pause and Lally imagined Effie removing her shoes, worn into a pleated round-toed shape as if she had unnaturally foreshortened feet. A pause while she put on her slippers and then Effie burst into the kitchen, '*Do not forsake me, oh my darling,*' accompanying her in a series of chortles and breathy bursts of song.

'Good film, Effie?'

'Oh, it was wonderful, my lover. Gary Cooper reminds me so much of your daddy and Grace Kelly is just a dream – so beautiful.' Effie stopped and looked closely at Lally. 'Do you know, I believe you resemble her. Yes, I really believe you do. "*An ice maiden with hidden depths of fire.*"'

'Where on earth did you get that from, Effie?' Lally was gratified but determined not to show it.

'*Picturegoer*. It wrote that she was "an ice ma . . ."'

'Yes, you said.' Lally licked her finger and pressed it into the crumbs of chocolate on her plate, the last smudge of sweetness licked from her skin. 'Effie?'

'Yes, my lover.'

'I had a little accident while you were out.' Lally arranged her face into an expression that she hoped would underline her resemblance to Grace Kelly, *distinguée* but vulnerable, and looked at Effie.

'Did you hurt yourself? Are you all right?' The humming stopped and Effie's eyes were magnified anxiety behind her glasses.

'I was in Mummy's room looking for something she wanted and I picked up St Antony.' Lally paused, long enough for Effie to understand that Lally had been in no way negligent, that the statue had in some mysterious movement leapt from her hands and dashed itself to pieces in the grate. 'I was asking him to help Mummy get better – you know how she thinks he can work a miracle any time she asks – and,' she faltered, 'I dropped him and he smashed to smithereens. Oh, Effie, what shall I do? Mummy'll be so upset.'

'Where are the pieces? Perhaps we can mend him so that she doesn't notice.'

'In the dustbin. It wouldn't be any good anyway because there weren't even two bits big enough to stick together. She really loved that statue; what am I going to say to her?'

Effie sat down next to Lally and looked towards the window as if it were a cinema screen on which Gary Cooper might appear, unarmed, from the shadows and deliver the answer. Autumn had been late in overtaking summer and it was not really dark even now. Trees and bushes shone silvery grey in the long twilight but only a reflection of the green shaded light showed on the glass.

'Best to tell her all the same. It'll be worse if she just finds out.' Effie was no longer singing, remembering Coral's displeasure when a favourite cranberry glass had been damaged some years before. Coral had taken the value of the glass out of Effie's already inadequate wages at half-a-crown a week, but far worse than the hardship this had caused were the abusive silences and accidental collisions which Effie endured until her penance had been discharged. It was a time on which Effie chose not to dwell and now she looked at Lally, knowing what was expected of her. 'I'll tell your mother that I did it while I was dusting. How will that do?'

'Oh no, Effie, I can't let you do that. *I'll* tell Mummy.

I'll tell her tomorrow when I go in to show her my new dress.' Lally put a hand on Effie's arm. 'She won't say anything in front of other people will she?' Effie shook her head and Lally continued, 'We'll have to try and find another St Antony though, before she comes home. I'll ask Mother Immaculata. I expect there's one tucked away at St Perpetua's somewhere that they'll let us have. Don't worry about it anymore, Effie, it'll be all right.' Lally got up leaving the remains of her meal for Effie to clear away, pleased that the evening which had promised so little had turned out so much better than she could have expected. Lally didn't even wonder why Billy had not come home.

'Teresa often used to wear a hat didn't she?'

'No, it was Maureen who wore the hats and Teresa who had the *mantilla*. Don't you remember when it caught fire one year at Candlemas?'

'I'd forgotten.' Coral smiled at the memory of the young woman snatching a burning veil from her head, the smell of singeing, as the congregation sang on regardless. Lally had been five or six at the time and hardly to blame if the candle she held had tilted in her small hand.

'I saw them at the fishmonger's this morning. Buying pieces for the cat they said, but I know they haven't had a cat since their Benbow died. Must be in low water, poor old girls. Asked to be remembered to you.' Billy watched Coral for her reaction but he could see that her attention had strayed from the fate of the Driscoll sisters and he waited for the litany of complaints to begin again.

'What were you doing in the fishmonger's? It's not Friday.'

'Saw some dab in the window and just thought how nice they'd be with some brown bread and butter.'

'Better than we get in here. Last night the liver was so tough I couldn't chew it at all, and the stewed fruit was full of bits of goodness-knows-what.' Coral's face puckered with self-pity and Billy allowed his thoughts to return to Teresa Driscoll. Not as attractive as her younger sister, her face beginning to lose its firm contours, her hair even blacker than it had been years ago when they first became acquainted and Billy had realised that here was a woman who appreciated men.

Billy was thinking about Teresa when the door opened and Lally came into the room behind an old woman who bore a striking resemblance to Miss Hawkey who occupied the bed opposite to Coral. Lally hesitated, waiting for her mother to realise that she was there, but it was Billy who stood up and went to fetch a second chair, kissing Lally on the cheek as he passed.

'Turn around. And again. I still can't see your feet, you'll have to stand further out.' Lally moved a yard nearer the other beds, smiling apologetically at Miss Hawkey who was up and sitting in a chair next to her sister, both women listening to Coral performing for their benefit. Coral searched for something to say. 'I don't understand why you always have to choose such dreary colours. A young girl like you can wear any shade and get away with it. You take Mrs Spargo over there in the corner; her two granddaughters came to visit her and they wore salmon-pink and a lovely electric-blue and they looked so fresh and pretty. Why can't you be more like them?'

Lally had seen Mrs Spargo's granddaughters giggling together out on the fire escape as they smoked forbidden cigarettes. 'All right then?' Salmon-Pink had called after her, and Electric-Blue had added, 'You look some smart, going somewhere nice?' Lally had smiled and hurried on, conscious of the unsuitability of grey silk in the afternoon, unwilling to explain her appearance to the two mocking faces which followed her progress down the corridor.

'You don't like my dress.' It wasn't a question.

'I didn't say that. It's better than I was afraid it might be.' Coral was grudging, 'I expect it's just blown together though, from a shop like The Bandbox, but it does do something for you, I must say that, gives you a bit of shape.'

'Well, I think you look lovely, my dear.' The visiting Miss Hawkey put out a hand to touch the heavy ribbed silk of Lally's dress. 'Grey suits you so well; you look like a dear little pigeon.' Lally turned towards the two old women and was disconcerted by a wink from a faded blue eye. 'And I just love your shoes.' Lally looked down at her feet; softest pearl grey kid on a Louis heel, which had cost almost as much as the dress. 'I had a pair very like them when I was your age. In fact we both did, do you remember Pru?' Patience Hawkey turned to her sister and then looked back at Lally. 'We're twins, you see, and we were always dressed exactly alike. I don't think that's approved of these days — supposed to repress individuality or some such theory, but we didn't know about all that and it doesn't seem to have done us much harm.' She smiled the charming smile that hid the apprehension she felt at her inability to allay her sister's illness. 'You'll be the belle of the ball, my dear, just you remember that and next time we meet I want to hear *all* about it.'

Billy scraped his tinny chair on the floor and Lally moved back to her mother's side, reluctant to leave the two old women, Patience and Prudence, who always joked that they had been given the wrong names and who answered to either.

Coral smoothed imaginary wrinkles from the bell-shaped skirt that swung around Lally's slender legs, finding an imperceptible fault in the neckline to rearrange. 'If I wasn't stuck in here I could have helped you to choose something gayer, younger, but I suppose it will have to do.' Coral lay back as if she were exhausted and Lally looked dispassionately at her mother's face, aware that there had been a change in her but unable to determine just what it was.

'I'm afraid we'll have to go,' Billy said. 'I've got to get this young lady home before the clock strikes six and my car turns back into a pumpkin.'

'I hear that you're taking Teresa Driscoll with you tonight and who's this Davy Hosegood?' Coral opened her eyes again but her voice was quiet, her hands picking at the washed-out blanket on her bed, over and over as if she were plucking feathers from a carcass.

Billy's expression gave nothing away. 'Davy's a new customer at the Bank; coincidence really as I was at school with his brother years ago. Davy went to Oxford and then into the army but now he's thinking of coming back to Penalverne and he's looking around for somewhere to buy. Could do the Bank some good so I thought I'd introduce him to the club, and Teresa seemed a good idea as a partner.'

'He's not married then?'

'Not as far as I know.'

'Oh.' Coral's mouth showed deliberation but she said nothing more. Billy leaned over her and kissed her on the cheek. He seemed not to notice that she ignored him and only lifted her face to accept Lally's goodbye.

Lally turned at the door to see Patience and Prudence Hawkey watching her. Patience gave another sketchy wink and Lally smiled back before walking lightly down the corridor to freedom with her father.

'I've run your bath for you. Come down in your dressing-gown for something to eat and then I'll help you to dress.' Effie slipped the grey silk dress on to a hanger of padded gold sateen which she hung behind the door in Lally's bedroom. 'If you pass me your shoes I'll give them a bit of a rub up.'

'There's no need, Effie, they're not marked, but you could find me some clean white gloves and my pearls and I suppose I should take a handbag. The little lizard-skin one will do.' Lally sounded tired and Effie watched her as she eased down her stockings and allowed her pale cream petticoat to slide to the floor, where it lay like a fallen flower.

'Didn't Madam like the dress then?' Effie bent down to retrieve the slip.

'She didn't say either way really, but apparently it would have been more appropriate for me to wear something brighter – salmon-pink and electric-blue were mentioned.' Lally gave a half-smile and sat down on the edge of the bed, her shoulder blades like two sharp little wings on either side of the too prominent bones in her spine, her ribs visible and affecting. Effie sat down beside Lally and Lally, afraid that their flesh would touch, moved slightly to increase the distance between them.

'Was that all?' Effie was rolling the discarded stockings, careful not to snag the nylon with her rough hands. Lally looked down at her own hands, pale pink nails and the softest, whitest skin, unmarked by any unwonted labour. The aquamarine ring that Billy had given her gleamed on her right hand and she turned it round and round trying to find the words which would enable Effie to understand that she knew that there was something wrong with Coral: that she, Lally, had noticed a change in her to which Billy seemed oblivious.

'Better have that bath before it gets cold.' Effie's voice intruded on Lally's thoughts. 'I'm going down to make your bread and milk. You need something like that if you're going to be eating all those little bits and pieces; no goodness in any of them and you look as if you could do with a bit of feeding up.' Effie put her hand on Lally's thigh and Lally shuddered. 'I'd not noticed how thin you've gone — you're not trying those tricks again are you? You promised last time that you'd eat properly. It's all very well for those nuns to deny themselves but they're not growing girls and I don't know what Mother Immaculata thinks she's up to, encouraging you in all kinds of nonsense.'

'I'm eating tons and it's got nothing to do with Mother Immaculata. I've lost a bit of weight since I started my secretarial course and Mummy's been ill, that's all. It's probably worry, you know how it is.' *Why can't she leave me alone? And please don't let her touch me again, I'm not a child anymore and I have to control my appetite or I'll end up like my mother and I'd rather die than be like her. No! No! I don't mean that. I love her, I really do, but I don't want to have something wrong with my gall bladder, that's all I meant, nothing else. Nothing.* Lally took her dressing-gown from Effie and rubbed cold cream into her face, just as Coral had taught her. 'I won't be long.' She forced herself to sound normal. 'I'm looking forward to the slingers.' Lally used the local name for bread and milk to make Effie smile. 'Lots of nutmeg and sugar?'

Lally snuggled into the soft velvet folds of her dressing-gown and padded down the passage to the bathroom. The steam rising from the water smelled of roses and Lally realised that Effie must have been lavish with Coral's bath essence. She allowed herself to lie full length in the water, closing her eyes and asking herself once again why Mother Immaculata had warned against the temptation inherent in this indulgence.

Lally had begun to wonder lately if her thoughts were audible: if Effie heard her arguing with herself against eating as much as she wanted; if Coral listened to Lally assuring the voice how much she loved her mother, or if Billy were able to eavesdrop on the thoughts in her head when she stood compliantly by his side, saying aloud what was expected of her. 'Yes, thank you, my mother is much better, we're hoping that she'll be home soon.' 'Oh, I don't know about Daddy being lucky to have me as a partner, it's great fun for me too.' Words that no-one listened to in any case, inconsequential chatter to Billy's odd little daughter, gossip to be exchanged over the sherry and pink gins in the drawing rooms of Penalverne and dismissed with a knowing smile.

Lally dried herself with the thick white towel that Effie had laid out for her and then removed the cream from her face, splashing her skin with cold water, just as her mother had instructed. Back in her bedroom she cleaned her nails and brushed her hair, wild and springy from the steam of the bath water, and went downstairs to a bowl of bread and milk. Lally, at nearly eighteen, could have been six years old and making ready for bed, not preparing for an evening as consort to her father among people to whom she was an anomaly, a fact of which she was well aware.

CHAPTER EIGHT

'Awfully dull for a young woman like you.' Davy Hosegood's face loomed close to Lally. She could see the dark shadow on his jaw, faint etched craters of boyhood acne. He smiled, unaware that a piece of parsley was wedged in his teeth. Lally smelled on his breath the shrimps which had filled a vol-au-vent, half of which lay, uneaten, on his plate. His smile was kindly and Lally was caught off guard.

'My mother says that it's good for me to meet people, that it will make me get over my shyness, and I am getting used to it a bit.' Lally took a little of her drink and showed it to Davy. 'It's only tonic water but I expect everyone thinks it's gin.'

'You don't like gin?'

'I only tried it once and I thought it was disgusting. Actually,' Lally lowered her eyes and Davy noticed how her hands tightened on her glass, 'I've tried most things but I didn't like anything. Except rum, and that only a little, so I decided it was easier not to drink alcohol at all.' Lally sipped nervously as if she would have recalled the words spoken so freely to a stranger. She was surprised to hear herself continue, 'I wonder sometimes if that means I shouldn't eat truffles or liqueur chocolates although I do like those. What do you think, Mr Hosegood?'

Davy looked directly at Lally and she lowered her eyes again. 'Won't you call me Davy? Mr Hosegood makes me feel old and sensible and I'm not actually either. As to your question, first of all, where on earth do you manage to find such things as truffles? The most I ever manage to find these days is a quarter of coughdrops.'

Lally looked at Davy as if she didn't understand his question. 'Mummy always has chocolates. It never occurred to me to wonder where they came from. Oh dear,' suddenly she understood, 'it was the black market wasn't it?'

'Don't worry about it, it was only a joke.' Davy looked at Lally's face, which was full of sudden concern. 'Not a very good one, I admit and nearly everyone did bend the rules about rationing a bit in the war you know.'

'All the same she's always been very critical of people who did and it's not very honest is it?'

'Not your problem. As to your original question, I don't think it counts if they're classified as sweets. Perhaps it might if you were TT on principal but if you like, say, cherry brandy in chocolate, I think you might count yourself absolved from your resolution. Does that satisfy you?'

Lally, who usually said on these occasions no more than was demanded by politeness and then in the most practised of clichés, looked at Davy Hosegood with gratitude. 'That's a very reassuring answer. Thank you, Davy.' *Guard your eyes. Guard your eyes, Lally, you don't want him to see that you like him. You mustn't allow him to think that you are a girl who seeks the company of men, that you want him to go on talking to you.* 'And now I'd better go and look for my father, if you'll excuse me.'

As Lally turned towards the middle of the room to search for Billy, Davy Hosegood put a hand on her arm and turned her towards him again. Lally shivered but the hand was not withdrawn. 'I think I heard your father say that he had some business to attend to and I'd be glad of your company. Odd man out tonight as I don't know anyone so it's a privilege to be with the prettiest girl in the room.'

Lally faced Davy. 'You've got parsley stuck in your teeth.' Her tone was unmannerly, dismissive, but Davy laughed and ignored what she had said. 'I'm sorry, that was rude.' Davy removed his hand from Lally's arm and her panic retreated. 'Do you think we could find some food, I'm quite hungry?'

'Come with me; I always believe in making a recce of the refreshments well in advance and there were some half-decent nibbles but don't attempt the vol-au-vents —

they're quite, quite dreadful.' Chattering quietly, Davy led Lally to the committee room where tables had been laid with plates of workmanlike sandwiches and cakes whose decoration owed more to enthusiasm than finesse. Lally wanted to giggle and looking at Davy she saw that he understood. They found asparagus and ham rolled in brown bread which was cut so thinly as to be almost transparent and they filled their plates, turning away to conceal from the club secretary their rapacity, before moving to the deep window seat that overlooked floodlit, dewy grass.

'Mr Hosegood? Sorry, Davy?'

'Mmmm?' Davy's mouth was full of food.

'Daddy said he was at school with your brother.'

'Quite right. My *older* brother.' He looked speculatively at Lally. 'You want to know how old I am, don't you?' Lally blushed, cornered, while Davy watched her quite openly. 'I'm thirty-seven and, if you don't mind my saying so, your blush is absolutely captivating. A sort of pink glow that makes you look less apprehensive and even prettier than before.'

Lally didn't know what to say. Her father's friends spoke to her of the weather, of her plans for the time when she would have completed her secretarial training. More recently, of course, they had enquired after her mother's health, and to all these approaches Lally had replied with politeness, words that were forgotten as soon as the questioner moved away to join his own circle, to flirt, to exchange gossip unsuitable for a girl of Lally's age. Now, Davy Hosegood, unattached and unfamiliar, had singled her out and Lally felt the danger of which she had so often been warned, the ease with which she could be seduced by someone who listened to her, who met her as an equal.

'You were right about the vol-au-vents, they're frighteningly pink, aren't they?'

'They taste even pinker than they look, but these are good.' Davy held up his plate. 'I suppose someone bottled the asparagus but they're really quite acceptable wouldn't you say?' Lally, unaccustomed to being asked what she thought of anything, ducked her head and took another bite of her roll but Davy continued quietly, persistently. 'I'd value your opinion, Lally, what do you think?'

'I think they're very good – perhaps a little too soft.'

'Excellent. Just what *I* thought.' Davy seemed inordinately pleased with Lally's reply. They ate in silence for a while but Lally felt none of the unease she had come to associate with the immediacy of men; no disquiet waiting for an arm to encircle her body, no misgiving expecting a hand to caress her thigh. Davy watched Lally relax and then spoke again, gentle, perceptive. 'Your opinion is just as valuable as anyone else's you know. More than a lot of people's, I expect, as you do actually think about things, I can see that.' He waited, watching her, until Lally was forced to reply.

'I suppose I do. Too much sometimes, as Mother

Immaculata's always saying that I'm scrupulous, although I don't understand why that is wrong.'

'Why don't you ask her what she means?'

'I suppose ... I think ... that I'm not used to questioning what is said to me. Mother Immaculata implied that having scruples is wrong so I just accepted it. It's what I do, you see, accept things.' Davy heard the pain in Lally's voice but he resisted the impulse to try to comfort her. Instead he stood up and suggested that they dance.

'If you like we could try a quickstep although I ought to warn you that I'm the world's worst dancer. Do you feel like taking me on?' Lally put down her plate and wiped her fingers on a handkerchief edged with Effie's hand-made lace. 'I have a feeling that you're a good dancer and I will try not to step on your toes.'

Lally looked down. Davy was wearing a pair of very old-fashioned patent leather evening shoes, the toes pointed and narrow, the leather cracked where it joined the sole. He followed her gaze. 'My father's. He's the only other person I know who wore fifteens. Huge, aren't they?' He slipped a hand under Lally's elbow and moved towards the sound of music. Bob Starr and The Constellations launched into *Muskrat Ramble* and Davy's long, shiny shoes wove a pattern of complicated sequences which Lally followed, allowing herself to lie easily in his arms and to be guided by his practised competence.

It was while The Constellations were playing *Red Sails in the Sunset* that Lally became aware of faces turned towards her and that her father was looking in the direction of the table where she sat with Davy drinking ginger ale. 'I expect they'll think it's whisky,' he had said, 'and surmise that I've corrupted you.'

Lally tried to think of a suitable reply but she was unequal to the demands of repartee and remained silent, smiling at Davy to show that she understood his joke. Davy, for his part, had seen the anxiety that surrounded Billy spreading like waves as he walked towards the table. Davy moved closer to Lally, only just restraining himself from putting a protecting arm around her as watchful eyes nudged Billy onwards. Davy stood up and pulled out a chair for the older man, who sat down heavily as if he were very tired.

'Having a good time, darling?'

'Oh, I am. I really am, Davy's a wonderful dancer.'

'Good, good, that's what I like to hear.' An almost imperceptible look passed between the two men. 'Lally,' Billy said, 'I hate to break up the evening as you're enjoying it so much, but there's a bit of bad news I'm afraid I have to tell you.' The light went out of Lally's face and she looked pinched and fearful as if anticipating her father's next words. 'I've just had a telephone call to say that Mummy's had a small stroke.' He put his hand on hers as if to stifle the sound that Lally was, in any case, incapable of making. 'The doctors say that it's not too bad but I think we ought to go home. I'll go on to the hospital and ring you as soon as I know anything more.'

'I knew,' Lally whispered. 'I knew something was wrong when I saw her this afternoon but I didn't say anything. It's my fault isn't it? I should have told someone. Oh, Daddy, she's not going to die, is she?' *Please don't let her die* . . .

'Hush, Lally, hush. Of course Mummy's not going to die. Once she's over this she'll be as good as new and we must do all we can to help her.'

Davy was watching Billy and saw a face which was a map of tantrums endured, of threats sustained, and wished for his sake that the outcome of Coral's latest disorder would be conclusive. His voice sounded unexpectedly positive. 'You go straight to the hospital, Billy. I'll get a taxi and take Lally home and drop Teresa off on the way.'

'I'd forgotten Teresa.' Billy looked around him but the concern with which he had been surrounded was already dissipating, replaced in the minds of the indifferent by more exciting and far less benevolent speculation.

'Not to worry, I'll find her. You just get off and I'll make sure everyone gets home safely.' Billy leaned forward and kissed Lally on the cheek, disturbed at the misery on her face. He patted Davy on the shoulder and was lost amongst the crowd. Davy helped Lally to her feet. 'Find your coat, Lally, and meet me by the door in ten minutes.' Davy spoke with authority and Lally moved away towards the ladies' cloakroom without a word.

Teresa Driscoll was standing in front of the long glass which hung over a row of basins, shaping her eyebrows with a small, black brush. She smiled at Lally. 'Cheer up, chicken, it may never happen.'

'Hello, Teresa. Davy's looking for you – he's taking us home.' It was all Lally could do to say the words aloud and Teresa, exchanging the brush for a worn enamel lipstick case, understood at once that something was wrong. 'Why's Davy taking us home – is there something wrong with your father?'

There was a chair in the corner of the cloakroom. Gold paint had flaked from its frame and one of the struts on the back had been mended inexpertly with glue that bulged and beaded like resin from a tree trunk. On the accompanying Lloyd Loom table there was a saucer, holding a few threepenny bits and two sixpences. Next to the saucer was a pincushion stuck with several needles threaded ready for repairs and a card of hairgrips, brown and white. Lally sat down as carefully as an old woman and looked at the table without seeing it. Much later on she found that she was able to recall in accurate detail each element of its commonplace little tableau.

'Your father, Lally, why isn't he taking us home?' Teresa's voice was kind but insistent.

'He's gone to the hospital. To my mother.' Lally looked at Teresa. 'My mother's had a stroke and if she dies it'll be my fault. I shall have been responsible for her death.'

Teresa lit a cigarette, standing under a notice

requesting members to kindly refrain from smoking in the cloakroom, screwing up her eyes against the smoke. 'Of course you're not; how can you even think such a thing? No, don't tell me,' Teresa tapped ash into the nearest basin, 'you've been listening to Mother Immaculata for far too long. That old dame nearly got me too when I was your age, but I discovered the fleshpots of Penalverne just in time.' Teresa took another long drag from her cigarette. She had soft, dark brown eyes that concealed, not deep thoughts, well-constructed calm, but an almost total lack of conviction on any subject. Now she looked at Lally's white face and said more gently, 'Where are we supposed to meet Davy?' Before Lally could answer Teresa looked around vaguely and said, 'Have you seen my other earring? I took them off to rest my ears as they pinch like hell and I thought I'd left them on the table but there's only one there now.' Lally made a token show of looking around her and Teresa said, 'Never mind, it doesn't matter as we're in a rush – I expect it's fallen on the floor and the cleaner will find it in the morning. I lose earrings all over the place but these are quite pretty, sparkly, and it's annoying to have only one – I'd rather lose both really.'

'We're to meet Davy at the entrance. He's getting a taxi and I think we should go as he said ten minutes.' Lally stood up, the grey dress a little wrinkled from where she had been sitting awkwardly on the gold-painted chair. Teresa shrugged herself into her own Persian lamb coat, handing Lally the little fur cape and together they made their way to the front of the club house. Lally's hand, deep in the pocket of her dress, was clasped around stones that stood proud of their cheap setting but which were, as Teresa had said, sparkly and desirable.

'Pull the sheet tighter on your side, my lover, we don't want wrinkles.' Effie tucked starched and ironed cotton under the mattress of Coral's bed. The bed had been brought downstairs and stood in a small room which Billy had used as his retreat from the household of women in which he lived. His books still stood on the shelves but the old leather armchairs had been removed and a heavy roll-topped desk had been pushed against the wall to make room for Coral's divan. Effie had arranged Coral's bedside table exactly as she liked it and Lally had done her best to make a butler's tray into an acceptable dressing-table, her mother's cut-glass bottles and pots of cream and nail polish arranged just as they had always been.

Several vases of flowers brightened the corners of the room and Lally had gathered cushions from around the house, placing them carefully in an attempt to disguise what was essentially an austere and masculine sanctuary. A new St Antony, smaller and brighter than his predecessor, stood in concealing shadow on the mantelpiece, a gift from Mother Immaculata.

Effie ran her hands over the smooth blankets and

turned down one corner of the sheet, moving as she did so, a monstrous Spanish doll with skirts of frilled scarlet taffeta that was almost as old as Lally but whose flossy black hair and tasselled shawl showed little signs of wear. Effie looked around her and sighed. 'My dear life, who'd ever have thought it would come to this?'

Lally leaned against a stool at the foot of the bed. 'It's not so bad, Effie, and the flowers jolly it up a lot. It's only for a while after all, and once Mummy's walking better she can go back to her own room. The only thing is the smell in here: it still smells like Daddy's room and I don't know how to get rid of it.'

'Squirt a drop of scent around the place. Here.' Effie handed the glass bottle to Lally and Lally felt the rubber bulb in its crocheted cover in her hands. She handed it back to Effie.

'You do it. I'm going to fetch Mummy's crucifix, she'll worry if that's missing.' Lally climbed the staircase in the quiet house, stepping lightly on the treads, crossing the landing to her mother's room. She lifted down the crucifix and, standing in the hollow, deserted room, Lally felt as she had as a small child concealing the knowledge of an alien presence in the house, hearing the confusing cries as if her mother had been hurt and she thought now with revulsion of the command to open the windows and to spray the air to clear away the cigarette smoke that lingered in the bedroom and the promises extracted not to worry Daddy about the headaches that struck so unpredictably in the afternoons and which caused Coral to moan with untold pain.

That was all my fault too, I could have stopped it. I should have told someone but that would have made Daddy sad and Mummy ill and angry with me. But she's ill anyway and it's all because I wanted her to die. I didn't love her enough and now she's really ill. But I don't want her to die, I truly don't, and I did try not to allow those thoughts to come into my head. I did try, I really did my best but it wasn't good enough. Nothing ever is good enough.

'Lally, Lally, hurry, they're here.' Effie was calling up the stairs and Lally carried the crucifix down to the makeshift bedroom, putting it carefully in the middle of Coral's night table.

Lally watched Billy and Effie helping Coral out of the car and into the wheelchair which had been strapped half-in and half-out of the boot. Coral reminded Lally of a doll that Effie had made her long ago, whose lumpy arms and legs had been fashioned from the unworn parts of pink rayon petticoats and whose attachment to the body was loose and always suspect. Effie had unravelled an old cardigan of Coral's, discarding the felted wool patches under the arms, to make flowing copper-coloured hair which was confined in two braids and tied with ribbons that matched a dress made from scraps of Lally's old skirts. Lally had called this grotesque figure Princess Pansy and had subjected it to every assault her childish mind could design, reverting to maternal concern whenever Effie was watching her.

As Coral settled into the chair Lally saw how Billy lifted one of her legs onto the footrest and laid an arm across her lap, where Coral cradled it as if to protect a small pet from uncalled for attention. The Princess Pansy face looked soft like dough that had risen and collapsed, one eyelid declined, one side of the mouth no longer firmly closed. Lally tried to ignore the slight trickle of saliva that escaped and at which Coral dabbed with one of Billy's large, white handkerchiefs.

As soon as Coral was wheeled into the room prepared for her Lally knew that it was a mistake. Coral's one good eye saw, not the carefully thought-out arrangement of her more personal possessions nor the flowers and bright cushions, but Billy's desk, dark and cumbersome, his books and the photographs of his family which had been banished from the rest of the house at an earlier stage of the marriage.

Coral struggled to speak but Lally, leaning close to her mother, could make out no more than, 'Upstairs. Pictures.' It was Effie, whose own speech was so indistinct as to be almost incomprehensible to outsiders, who seemed to understand from the first exactly what Coral was striving to convey. Effie helped Coral into bed, Billy standing ineffectually beside her. He took possession of the wheelchair, glad of something to do, and pushed it into a recess beside the fireplace.

Coral tried to talk and an excited Effie interrupted her song to say soothingly, 'Don't fret, my bird, I'll move the chair outside drec'ly. You just settle down and I'll bring you a nice cup of tea – I don't suppose you've had a decent cup since you went into hospital.'

Lally had been unpacking her mother's small suitcase, placing her hairbrush and comb on the improvised dressing-table, glancing into, and quickly away from, a linen bag of dirty washing, when the telephone rang and she hurried into the hall to answer it. Lally repeated the number but there was no answering voice so she put down the receiver and went into the kitchen to make the tea that Effie had promised Coral. It wasn't the first time that the telephone had remained mute when Lally had answered it and she was coming to the conclusion that it was more than a coincidence and wondered if she should report a fault on the line.

Lally made the tea and put the teapot on a tray that Effie had left ready, thin bread and butter covered with the waxed paper which had once lined a box of cornflakes. As Lally carried it toward Coral's room Billy came towards her looking disconsolate. 'It's going to be more difficult than I feared,' he said. 'We've obviously got it wrong. Thought your mother'd like to be downstairs and it would be much easier for Effie, but tomorrow we'll have to move everything back the way it was and between us we'll move your mother upstairs somehow.' He looked at Lally. 'Was that the phone I heard?'

'A wrong number, I think. At least, no-one answered.' Billy made a noise like a grunt, placed his hand on Lally's shoulder and wandered off towards the room at the front of the house wishing he could go to the golf club but unsure of what reception such a move would provoke. He wished that Teresa wouldn't telephone him at home: Lally hadn't said anything but he was sure that she was suspicious, preferring to dismiss the silent calls as a defect in the system rather than a failing in her father's probity. Billy decided to walk to the public call-box around the corner and speak to Teresa from there. He would tell her that he had to stay in with Coral this evening but what he would never tell her was that the sight of his wife, livid and slack-mouthed and unintelligible, he found odious, offensive to both his eyes and his ears. If one thing grieved Billy more than his inability to accept Coral transformed, it was the sight of her lustrous copper hair now lank and faded as if it were an allegory of the changes they would all have to accept.

If Billy had truly loved his wife, he knew that his feelings would be different but only the sight of Coral's hair, of which she had always been so proud, now both drab and grey and gathered into a loose and unbecoming bun touched his heart in a way that he had almost forgotten. It reminded Billy of the time when Lally had been born, so fragile and insubstantial, that he was afraid of hurting her, of wounding something so defenceless. Now it was Coral and Billy knew that her vulnerability was the surest shackle needed to keep him by her side.

With a sigh Billy picked up his car keys and went

outside to move the car and to telephone Teresa from the call-box while, inside the house in Advent Gardens, Lally fed her mother with slivers of bread and butter and Effie tried to teach Coral how to drink without spilling most of the liquid from her lopsided mouth.

CHAPTER NINE

The frost was so thick that at first glance the trees seemed covered with blossom. Against the clearest blue sky an illusion was given of spring but seed heads and grasses crumbled like glass at the lightest touch and the ground was rutted and frozen, each hoof print, each little puddle rimed with ice. Such a hard frost was unusual so close to the sea and it seemed to have taken the woods unawares, a smell of old mushrooms lingering in the dark depths of the trees, scarcely diminished in the rare, crisp air.

Dorcas and Gerry leaned against a fallen tree in the woods where bluebells grew in the spring but which were carpeted now in a mulch of pine needles and rotting leaves.

'Did you see much of Lally at Christmas?'

'I saw her once or twice.' Gerry sounded reluctant. 'Usually after church. She seems awfully odd – well, odder – since her mother's been ill and she talks all the time about it being her fault almost as if she *wanted* it to be. I don't really understand her any more.'

'I never really did although our mothers tried so hard to force us to be friends. Poor Lally. They didn't come to stay this summer, of course, and I don't think she sees many people of her own age any more. Except when she comes here, and this Davy Hosegood – did you meet him?' Dorcas took a forbidden cigarette from the packet Gerry passed to her before handing it back and leaning towards her friend to share the same match.

'He's not the same age as Lally, Dorcas, didn't she tell you? He's twenty years older than her and although he's terribly nice it's as though something's missing. I don't know: I'm sure he's awfully fond of Lally but he treats her just as he treats her parents. There's no *spark* there at all.'

'Perhaps that's what she likes. Perhaps she feels safe with him.'

'And perhaps you understand her better than you think.' Gerry picked up a stick and threw it at the younger of the dogs. 'Stop that you disgusting creature.' She turned back to Dorcas. 'Eugene stood her for the dog last week but missed and now she doesn't know what to do with herself.' Dorcas, who disliked both dogs equally, could think of no reply and made a face at Gerry, who laughed. She stamped on her cigarette end. 'I'm getting cold, let's go on.' Gerry called the dogs who streaked past them, knowing they were going home.

The two girls walked in silence for a while, the woods around them full of tiny noises. Mossy broken branches lined the path and leaves, skeletal remains of the summer's canopy, hung, transparent, on spiders' webs and the dried, dead stems of foxgloves and drooping ash keys. The path widened into a dell surrounded by bramble bushes and it was here that Dorcas had picked the blackberries which she had turned into jelly, straining the juice through muslin fastened to the legs of an upturned stool, skimming and dispersing the scum which rose to the surface of the pan. She took great pleasure in the translucent amethyst jars which filled half of the slate shelf in the old dairy, her hard work in the autumn transformed into enough jelly to be served with Cream Teas throughout the following summer.

Now a reluctant sun was lighting diamonds to sparkle in the yellow, tired grass which lay at the centre of a little amphitheatre while in the shadows near the bushes the frost was still as white and wintry as a Christmas card. 'I wish we had more weather like this,' Gerry said. 'I love the cold, the frost, the warmth of the fire when we get back to the house.' She was wearing a curious hand-made hat of boiled wool which someone had brought back from Norway, and with her long red hair she looked like an illustration from *The Scandinavian Twins*. 'I tried to paint the view from my window this morning but I couldn't put down what I could see. It's so frustrating.'

'If I could do anything even a quarter as well as

you paint I'd be pleased. All I can do reasonably well is cook but I do enjoy that and I suppose it means that I'll always have a job as people have to eat.'

'Are you going to stay here, Dorcas? Don't you feel that you would like to get away for a bit, see other places?'

'I can always go away on holiday if I want to but I love it here. Right from the first time I saw Petty Place I felt at home, as if it's where I belong. I know it's not very enterprising of me but I'd be happy to stay here, just as I am now, with the guests to cook for, and the horses, and Eugene and Greg to take me out and you visiting as often as you do. My idea of heaven, really.'

Gerry looked at Dorcas. 'I hope you'll always feel like that,' she said, 'because no matter how sure you are of what you want it rather depends on other people, doesn't it? If other people's lives change, you may have to change too. Look at Lally: would you ever have imagined her teaching at the Cornish College of Knowledge?'

'The Cornish College of Knowledge? Oh, I see, the Commercial Academy. Well, yes, actually I can. You and I have always had a choice you see but Lally hasn't, not really because there's no way at all that Aunt Coral would let her go off on her own. It's almost as if she had the stroke *deliberately* to keep Lally manacled to her side. She'll never get away now, especially as she's going to stay at home and teach shorthand and typing.'

'It makes me want to shake her until her teeth rattle. She's much cleverer than either of us but now she'll end up with varicose veins and brown cardigans and not being able to control the girls who are there because they can't think of anything else to do until they get married.'

'But at least Aunt Coral will be happy.'

'And that, after all, is the only thing that has ever really mattered in the house in Advent Gardens.' Gerry slashed viciously with a dog lead at the stalk of a long dead cow parsley, watching with satisfaction as it tore across and folded over on itself.

'Do you think she'll marry Davy Hosegood?'

'No.'

'You're very sure.'

'Lally's in love with Eugene, surely you know that? She always has been, but Lally being Lally I'm sure it's not straightforward.'

'What about you, Gerry? What will you do when you finish your course? Throw off all restraint and live a wild, Bohemian life in a garret?'

Gerry laughed, her smile made charming by front teeth that looked flat and splayed, a characteristic which on anyone else would have seemed an imperfection, but which only increased her attraction. 'I'm beginning to know what I want to do and when I'm sure I'll tell you, Dorcas, but not yet.' She was suddenly serious. 'I don't want children of my own, you see. I've had to spend so much time helping to bring up my brothers and sisters that I feel as if I've done all that already.'

'Won't that be a problem for you? As a Catholic, I mean.'

Gerry looked ahead to where the path ended and the fields of her uncle's farm stretched ahead, glittering and furrowed where Eugene had ploughed in the stubble soon after harvest but which had not yet been harrowed. 'Oh, I'll think about that another day.'

'Like Scarlett O'Hara?'

'Just like Scarlett O'Hara. She had the right idea, don't you think? Too many decisions to make all at once at our age but one thing I have made up my mind about, and that's this joint party for all our birthdays.'

'Did you get a chance to ask Lally what she thought?'

'It didn't seem the right time somehow, it was all so gloomy there. Do you know I didn't see her father at all and Lally said that he's out most of the time but she's still expected to dress up like the fairy on the Christmas tree and go with him to all those dull, dull dinners. My mother said . . .' Gerry stopped.

'What did your mother say?'

'Perhaps I shouldn't repeat gossip but it *is* about Lally – in a way.' The yard was full of muddy cows waiting to be milked and the girls walked over the cattle grid rather than trying to open the gate against the crush of steaming, earthy bodies. 'Well, Mum said that she thinks that Billy Bassett has a girlfriend.'

Dorcas stopped in her tracks and looked at Gerry in astonishment. 'Everyone knows that. He's had a girlfriend for absolutely yonks and only Lally isn't aware of it. Why do you think Billy takes her as

cover to what he calls *functions*? And Aunt Coral, by
pretending she doesn't know and going along with it,
has a spy in the camp: she makes Lally go over and
over every conversation and quizzes her about who was
there and who danced with her father, who spoke to
him ...'

'... I think that's going too far, even for horrible
Coral.' Gerry was angrier than Dorcas had ever seen
her. 'How do you know all this, Dorcas?'

'Mummy and Vernon have never tried to hide it
from me. They often talk about it and I suppose I
thought that you must have realised too. You didn't
think, did you, that Lally actually *enjoyed* having to do
all that?'

'Well, I don't think Lally enjoys a lot of what she has
to do although I *have* always thought it rather odd that
her father takes her everywhere. Do you suppose,' Gerry
said, 'that Lally's really a surrogate wife? After all, for all
the time I've known them her mother has never really
been well and Lally seems just to do whatever anyone
else decides for her.' Gerry hooked her feet into a jack
and pulled off her wellington boots. 'Don't like to dwell
too hard on all that as it tends to suggest the murky once
you *really* think about it, wouldn't you say?'

Dorcas changed places with Gerry at the boot jack.
'I don't know what I think. I always used to feel sorry
for Lally but now I feel exasperated more than anything;
that she *still* goes on doing exactly what's expected of her.
No-one could say that you and I are terribly rebellious or

anything but we do have some say in what affects us, what we want to do.' As Dorcas stood her boots, neatly paired, against the wall the door opened and Eugene came in, cold air sidling with him into the warmth of the house. He was wearing a duffle coat and under it a jersey mainly of navy wool which his mother had knitted for him from oddments. A contrasting white neckband had become detached from the yoke and lay raggedly around Eugene's throat giving him the appearance of a raffish vicar.

They moved together into the kitchen where splits and cakes were piled on wire racks to cool and where the kettle steamed gently on the back of the Rayburn. Gerry pulled the kettle forward onto the hottest plate and found mugs and milk and sugar.

'We were just talking about our birthdays,' she said to Eugene, who was sprawling on a chair close to the range, feet stretched out to the heat. A cat had jumped onto his lap and he stroked it very gently between its ears. 'We haven't asked Lally yet but we – Dorcas and I – think it would be wonderful if you *really* don't mind sharing your twenty-first with us.'

'I don't mind.' Eugene smiled at Dorcas, his eyes very bright in his brown face. Eugene had blue eyes like any other, perhaps darker than most, but not large nor with a remarkable shape. Perhaps it was the way they reflected the light; perhaps, although it seemed unlikely, they were lit from within by some unguessed at strength of character, but Eugene Jarvie's eyes seemed to dazzle and bewitch. They were like spotlights that illuminated his face and gathered within their focus everyone who looked at him. Long after his charm had been forgotten and his secretive, knowing smile, people could always say, *Oh yes, the boy with the eyes.*

Now Dorcas felt herself enticed into Eugene's world and she glanced quickly at Gerry to see if she had noticed. Gerry appeared to have observed nothing out of the ordinary as she buttered splits for all of them, finding cherry jam in the cupboard and pouring hot water into the big brown pot.

'If that's what everyone else wants I don't mind sharing but Gerry's the one who might miss out, not having a twenty-first of her own in six months . . .'

'. . . We'd never get everyone together again so soon. It's difficult enough to do it once, especially with Aidan away. Besides, it's not going to be of great significance to me.' She stopped suddenly as if she had thought better of finishing the sentence and Eugene looked at her before gently pushing the cat off his lap and going to the sink to wash his hands.

They ate the still-warm splits, Dorcas and Gerry leaning against the Rayburn, licking jam from their fingers and flicking crumbs to the several cats who had materialised from dark corners to sit in an avaricious semi-circle at the girls' feet.

'What about Lally?' It was Eugene who spoke as he poured himself a second mug of tea, lacing it with sugar.

'What *about* Lally?'

'You said you haven't asked her yet so how do we know she'll make it a foursome? Under normal circumstances I'd have thought that her mother would have preferred to wait until Lally's twenty-first and then have a huge thrash for her alone. But the way things are—' Eugene shrugged and went towards the back door. He put on his muddy boots and reached for the duffle coat. 'I hope she'll agree; it wouldn't be the same without her. Work on her, Gerry, and insist that she brings her elderly admirer with her. I want to meet him, to see if he's good enough for dear little Lally.' With a smile Eugene let himself out into the yard where a pale half-moon hung theatrically in the darkening sky.

The cows had wandered by themselves into their accustomed stalls and stood patiently waiting their turn to be milked. Eugene turned the peak of an old tweed cap of his father's around to the back of his head and nudged into the snowflake-patterned side of a young heifer, listening to the steady splash of milk into Greg's bucket at the far end of the cowshed.

Since Aidan had left for the seminary Eugene and Greg had run the farm between them, deferring in most things to their father but more impatient than he was to expand and modernise. Eugene, if he thought about it at all, suspected that Greg was unhappy, only waiting for an opportunity to leave. They didn't talk about it, preferring to exaggerate their differences with their father rather than enter into a deeper discussion of where their lives were taking them, linked necessarily closely to each other in the daily routine of the farm.

The cowshed in winter had become a purgatory to Greg Jarvie: rising at five-thirty to make cocoa before shuffling across the yard in the dark to the shed where the only warmth was from the cows and having to wash their udders in cold water, the cloth clammy and freezing around his fingers, fumes rising from the soaked, overnight bedding strong enough to make his eyes water. He wanted to be able to stay in bed at least until it was light; to be warm enough and clean enough in winter and not to have to work in blazing sun in the summer, chaff and seed heads in his hair, his eyes, his clothes.

There had never seemed to be a choice for him, the oldest of the three brothers. Aidan had always been different and he had made his escape through religion and Greg thought that Eugene was content enough, but he, Greg, felt trapped by the demands of a daily routine which could only be circumvented by the most elaborate of arrangements. Greg knew that he would leave the farm as soon as an opportunity arose and he wondered if Eugene realised how he felt. Their father was still strong and active and between him and Eugene they should be able to manage. But not if Eugene married the fey little friend of Gerry's which, if Greg were not mistaken, was where his brother's thoughts had been leading him. If Eugene married Lally, if *anyone* married Lally, they would take on themselves the responsibility for someone else's happiness which would prove a burden too heavy, an obligation of duty too great, to allow a normal affinity to develop within the marriage.

Greg knew this and wished he could warn Eugene but banter and bickering had become the way in which they communicated and he sighed and squirted a stream of milk into the mouth of one of the ubiquitous cats. He carried the bucket to the dairy, pouring warm milk into the cooler, watching for a minute as it rippled downwards to drip through a muslin cloth into the churn. The dairy had the chill of the grave in the cold grey morning, slate shelves, wet concrete floor, whitewashed walls. Even the cowshed was slightly warmer and Greg turned, pouring onto an old tin lid the last of the milk in his bucket. He placed the makeshift bowl on a low wall outside the dairy for the wild kittens who would only appear if no-one was watching them.

Greg saw a light come on in the kitchen and knew that Gerry must be up. She was always the first to rise and by the time that he and Eugene came in for breakfast she would have bacon and eggs warming in the oven, sausages perhaps, and toast. He wished that she lived with them all the time and he wished even more that she was not his cousin. Suddenly Greg knew what was wrong with him and with that knowledge came discomfiture.

*　　*　　*

Dearest Lally,

This is from me and Gerry, acting under instructions from Eugene. We've been talking about our birthdays and someone — I've forgotten who and it doesn't matter anyway — suggested that instead of having four separate celebrations we should have one _huge_ party. What do you think? Isn't it a super idea?

We thought it could be in April as it will be Eugene's real twenty-first and he says he doesn't mind sharing with the rest of us as Gerry will be twenty-one in October anyway and our eighteenths are so close together and close to his birthday as well. Not that eighteen means anything special but we'd probably have had some kind of a party, wouldn't we?

We did think about having it here at PP but Eugene's parents say we can use the old barn and then there'll be plenty of room for food and dancing and anyone who wants to can sleep there if they want to stay on. Mummy says that A Coral and U Billy can stay with us so you needn't worry about them.

Dear Lally, _please_ say you agree. It wouldn't be the same without you, and Eugene has specifically said that he wants you to come. _And_ please bring Davy H with you — we're all _longing_ to meet him as he sounds terribly nice. Does your mother approve of him?

Here Dorcas broke off, wondering if she should mention Lally's mother, if her reference to Coral's approval would be misconstrued by Lally. She decided it would not and continued with her letter.

Greg has been very moody lately and I think he misses Aidan. He (Aidan, I mean) is getting leave to come for Eugene's birthday. It's after Easter so that's all right, apparently. You'll know what that means, I expect; something to do with not being able to come home in Lent. Gerry tried to explain but I don't really understand the concept of denial as I believe in taking every opportunity that presents itself.

Dorcas smiled to herself, thinking of long afternoons spent with Eugene in the hay loft watching spiders spinning delicate threads that enveloped the bodies of flies so securely; of rain silently turning the smeared glass in the windows into a pattern of molten grey; of barbs from hidden thistles in the dried summer grass prickling and scratching her bare skin. She thought of the sweet smell of the hay and the stamping and snuffling of Rafferty, the big red bull, as he curled his tongue around the hay in his manger while she and Eugene watched him through holes in the floorboards.

<u>Please</u> talk to A Coral about this party thing and let us know as soon as poss. with a list of everyone you want to ask as we need to send out invites and there's quite a lot to organise. (To start with the barn is <u>filthy</u> and we'll have to try and get rid of some of the rats at least.)

 Haven't seen you for ages, not properly I mean, so please, please come, Lal. And bring Davy.

  Tons of love,
Dorcas (and Gerry and Eugene) XOXOXOXO

PS Nearly forgot the date! 17 April
PPS Love to A Coral and U Billy

Dorcas licked the flap of the long envelope, the gum bitter on her tongue, and scribbled Lally's address on the front. If she hurried she could catch the midday post so that Lally would have the letter by the next day and would have no excuse not to answer over the weekend.

Since Lally had started her secretarial course there had been less time to visit Dorcas, what spare time there was being spent propitiating Coral. Coral had progressed to a halting walk, one foot seeming almost detached at the ankle, one arm inclined across her body. Her speech continued to be a little muddled, although it was improving, but it was still only Effie who had no difficulty at all in understanding her.

Lally's life had become structured in such a way that there seemed little time for anything except work. When she came home from the Commercial Academy she went straight to see how her mother was feeling, enquiring, but not listening closely to the answer, as to how Coral had passed her day. Before dinner Lally did her homework, conscientious as she had always been and determined to do well in the end of year exams. After dinner she read to Coral or wrote letters for her. Sometimes she escaped for an hour with the excuse that she must post the letters or that she needed some fresh air after a particularly strenuous day at the Academy. Coral would try to dissuade her but Lally had become skilled at appearing to listen to her mother whilst not actually seeming to hear her.

Coral would become agitated and Lally watched her covertly, declining to substitute the correct word for whatever inconsistency Coral offered. It was a contest of wills that Lally, had she seized the advantage, could have won except that the old, familiar knowledge of the insignificance of her life and the remorse for what she regarded as her fault, kept her dependent on her mother's approval.

It was Davy who encouraged Lally to resist Coral's more immoderate demands. 'Effie loves to feel indispensable, you know that. And, for whatever deluded reason of her own, she actually enjoys Coral being unpleasant to her.' He reached for Lally's hand. 'You know it's true so don't try to pretend it's not. Anyway, the table's booked for eight o'clock so you'd better go and get ready.' He stood up and went to find Effie, and Lally, not allowing herself to hesitate, went to change and to struggle with her hair.

Davy had taken to calling once or twice a week at the house in Advent Gardens, any interest in Teresa Driscoll long since abandoned for the pretence that it was. Often he stayed to share her dinner with Lally, who otherwise sat alone, Effie still cooking enough for Billy as well although he was seldom there to eat it. Coral had her supper in her bedroom so the deception that Billy came home for dinner every night was easy to perpetuate.

At the weekends Davy would meet Lally in church and together they would walk home after Mass, along the prom if the weather was good, hurrying through the back lanes under Davy's big, black umbrella if it was wet. They were some of the happiest times that Lally had known and it never occurred to her, forced as she had always been into the company of her elders, that they made an incongruous couple, the delicate young woman and the man just old enough to be her father.

Davy never harried her, never intruded or took advantage of her inexperience. He never kissed her, unless it was on the cheek occasionally, when it seemed appropriate; never touched her except in the most courteous way and never gave her the slightest *frisson* of apprehension that he had any intention of crossing the barrier that Lally had erected around herself, the boundaries of which remained unnamed.

Dorcas, and even Gerry, would have found Davy's restraint unusual and confusing but Lally saw nothing singular in their affectionate companionship. There were times when Davy seemed to understand the turmoil in Lally's mind and would, by some word or action, pre-empt the voice in her head, subduing the clamour until Lally was free of the tumult of words over which she seemed to have less and less control. For this alone she would have given freely of her time to Davy but he never imposed or asked her for more than she was willing to give.

In this restrained and unconventional manner Davy courted Lally without her ever being aware that this was what he was doing, her mind fixed with all its intensity, as it had always been, on Eugene.

Eugene has specifically said that he wants you to come. Lally read through Dorcas's letter for the second time, lingering over the words that told her all she wanted to know; that Eugene was ready to acknowledge that it was Lally he needed, Lally to whom he was ready to commit himself; that the pledge she had made to herself to guard Eugene against the occasions of sin was about to be redeemed.

It was a Friday morning, a day on which Lally would usually have been at the Academy, but she had a cold. A dry, irritating cough had made her throat raw and she found it painful to swallow. Her head felt thick, almost too heavy for her neck to support, and even her eyes felt full of grit as if she had stood on the beach while the wind swirled sand around her. Effie had made lime tea which she had sweetened with honey and Lally, uncomplaining, drank each cupful presented to her although she thought it tasted like wet silage. Lally had been uncomfortable all night and had woken as irritable as she ever allowed herself to be. Effie had ignored her assurances that she was quite well enough to go to the Academy and had telephoned to say that Miss Bassett would not be returning until she was well again.

Dorcas's letter lifted Lally's spirits more than aspirin and lime tea could ever have done and she decided to reply at once. First of all she telephoned Davy who said that nothing would please him more than to accompany Lally to Petty Place and how was she? Resting and keeping warm and doing all that Effie told her? Later that morning six yellow roses encircled with gypsophila were delivered and Lally wondered how she was going to explain to Davy that the sign which she had so long awaited had now been made manifest: that Eugene was ready to declare his love for her.

Eugene has specifically said that he wants you to come. Lally knew that Davy was sensitive to her conviction that she had to wait for the purpose of her life to be revealed to her and that two retreats in the novitiate of St Perpetua's had left her confused rather than resolved as to what that purpose would be. But now, with the arrival of Dorcas's letter, Lally was triumphant. She understood that God had chosen for her the one way she had hardly allowed herself to acknowledge. She was to become Eugene's partner in life, his support in times of weakness, his apologist, his lover, his wife. Lally wondered if it was asking too much of Davy to understand that she was fulfilling her destiny.

Lally opened her leather writing case and picked up her fountain pen. The headache which she had found so intrusive seemed very much better and she determined to walk to the postbox later on, evading Effie's watchful solicitude at a time when Lally knew that Coral would claim Effie's attention.

Coral's passage of days was returning to something resembling her old way of life but it was an imitation of that life, like a faded photograph in which the details were more remembered than perceived anew. She had a weakness in her arm that no amount of physiotherapy seemed able to moderate, a small difficulty with her balance and a more pronounced impediment in remembering what had been said to her only a short while before. With Effie to help her Coral managed very well except in the matter of controlling her temper when a word eluded her or a memory, perceived as almost tangible, became elusive to the point of distraction.

It was as if the stroke which had curtailed Coral's physical abilities had also diminished the discipline with which she had subdued those characteristics which belonged to the past; a certain roughness in her speech, a coarseness of expression which belonged to the girl growing up in the terraced house in a road at the wrong end of the town and which Coral had long ago pretended to forget.

When Coral became fractious and uncontrolled in her frustration Effie just sang more loudly and once or twice in desperation resorted to a smack on Coral's good arm, which seemed to quieten her and left Effie feeling no remorse. Coral had tried to tell Lally about this punishment but Lally had chosen to ignore her mother's complaints, choosing instead to follow Davy's advice to distance herself from Coral if she could, in order to be able to lead a life of her own. The misgivings she felt, the guilt which was never totally subdued, Lally buried as well as she was able under what she considered to be a brisk consideration of what was best for all of them.

✳   ✳   ✳

When Lally had finished her letter to Dorcas she put on her coat, tied a warm scarf around her head and quietly let herself out of the house. It was a soft, damp day, grey and threatening real rain before long, but to Lally it seemed as though a rainbow might suddenly shine through the clouds, as if the sombre air was alive with birdsong and that the gardens full of stringy winter plants blazed and dazzled with colour. *Eugene wants me to come. He specifically said he wants me just as I always knew he would. Oh thank you, God, for keeping me pure and showing me what you want me to do. Not long now and I'll be with Eugene for good and no-one will be able to come between us.*

Lally posted her letter and took a longer way home, hanging up her damp coat just in time to conceal from Effie that she had been out in the drizzly winter air, before going up to her mother's bedroom to advise her of the plans which Coral was in no position to resist. Lally wondered if she should mention Eugene other than as a host but decided to keep their secret to herself a little while longer; to examine it in all its implications and to allow herself to delight in the knowledge that she was going to marry the man she had loved from the first moment she had met him.

It had been the first time she had gone to stay with Dorcas at Petty Place, on a spring day when the hedges around the farm were full of primroses, bigger and more yellow than Lally had ever seen. Eugene had been dishevelled and unconcerned, laughing with his cousin Gerry, taking little notice of her two friends beyond noticing that one was dark and very tall for a girl and looked as if she might be good fun and that the other was pale and delicate and looked scared to death.

Now, six years later, Eugene knew that his first impressions of Dorcas and Lally had been right and that he was a bit in love with both of them and he accepted, with an unbecoming complacency, that they were both in love with him. The night of the joint party, Eugene thought, should prove interesting.

CHAPTER TEN

<hr />

'I'm so glad the girls are sharing their birthdays, just as they did so many times when they were small.' The recollection of those parties filled Alma with nostalgia and retained resentment but looking at Coral Alma reminded herself of how lucky she herself had been to find Vernon, to live in a house like Petty Place and to have a daughter as untroubled as Dorcas.

Alma had hoped that she might have more children and for a while, when she had first married Vernon, she had felt disappointment but never to such an extent that it had impoverished her life, and as the reputation of Petty Place spread, so Alma's free time was curtailed until she thought only rarely, albeit with a passing sadness, of the babies she might have had, remaining thankful for what she regarded as the blessing of Dorcas and pragmatically concentrating her energy on what was before her.

Dorcas and Vernon had from the first established an affinity so close that visitors to Petty Place who knew no better assumed them to be father and daughter. They shared a sense of humour that sometimes left Alma puzzled, isolated by their quick understanding, although as the years passed even she sometimes forgot that they had not always been a family. When Dorcas sold her grandmother's house Alma was happy for Vernon to invest the money for her and, with the same good sense that had prompted him to buy excellent furniture for the hotel, the capital was increasing exponentially. Dorcas showed no inclination to use any of the money or, indeed, seemed very interested in it.

Alma heard Coral's voice intruding on her contemplation of her own good fortune. 'Just as well; shan't be around when Mary Marigold is twenty-one.' Coral looked at Alma, tears filming her unaligned eyes. Coral's face, thickly masked with too pale a shade of powder, reminded Alma of a pierrot, her mouth an arc of discontent. Alma wanted to contradict that flat, uncompromising statement but found that she was unable to supply the words which would have dispelled their justification. Instead she put her hands around Coral's cold, pale fingers, the nails filed and painted by Effie so that all should seem as normal.

'None of us might be,' was the best Alma could manage. 'Let's just enjoy these few days and give the girls a good time, they're looking forward to it so much. I can hardly ever remember seeing Lally looking so happy and it's lovely having you and Billy here, we missed you both last year.'

The tears spilled from Coral's eyes, making tracks down her powdery cheeks. 'Last time,' she said. 'Last time we shall come.' Coral shook her head as if she had heard Alma's unspoken protestations. 'I know, so you needn't pretend but, Alma, I want you to do something for me. Can't trust Effie, and Billy – well ...' She stopped speaking, silence filtering and surrounding the two women like motes of dust in the air of a suddenly disturbed room.

'Of course, whatever I can.'

'Don't know what it is yet.' Coral had made no attempt to dry the tears on her cheeks and now, very gently, Alma leaned across and wiped them away. 'It's Mary Marigold. She'll have no-one to look after her and she does need someone. You're the only person I trust enough to do it. Will you look after her, Alma? Will you do it for me? Don't let Mother Immaculata get her even if it means her marrying Davy Hosegood.'

Alma was startled. 'Is she thinking of marrying him? I shouldn't have thought so from what I've seen of them together. He's nice, of course, but hardly husband material for someone like Lally, is he?'

'Better than the convent.'

'But, Coral, she's so young, there's no need to worry about that yet and surely she'll make up her own mind when the time comes?' Alma said nothing to Coral of the change she had noticed in Lally, a doggedness in her attempts to distance herself from her mother, which seemed to Alma to stem more from desperation than conviction. 'Of course I'll look after her; she's always been like a second daughter to me anyway, and Vernon and I love having her here.' The deluding words came easily.

Coral leaned back in the chair and closed her eyes. 'Thinking especially of when Billy marries Teresa Driscoll. That's when Lally will need you. She'll find it very hard to accept that her precious father has been playing around with that tarty piece and thinking I didn't know about it.'

'Oh, Coral, I'm sure that's not true, and even if it were surely you wouldn't tell Lally?' The lies came more easily now to Alma.

Coral's face, so blank and noncommittal since her stroke, took on a shadow of the expression that Alma remembered so well. 'Wouldn't I? Wait and see. Just wait and see.' Coral turned her head towards Alma. 'You've always been my only real friend, Alma, apart from Effie and she hardly counts, and you always were, even when we were girls.'

'It makes a difference, knowing someone for so long.' Alma spoke truthfully now, wondering if their friendship was no more than a certain loyalty learned over the passage of time.

'Knowing each other so well.' Coral looked as if she wanted to say more, as far as Alma could tell from the immobility of the features behind the camouflage of make-up. If there was anything further to be said it remained unspoken as Coral had slipped into sleep with the precipitation that had become habitual to her. Alma waited for a while, looking at the diminished body, grieving for the plump, pretty young woman she had known and mildly disliked for most of her life. She left Coral sleeping and went to look for Effie so that Coral should not be alone and dismayed when she awoke.

Gerry had climbed the tallest ladder to hang ivy from the beams in the barn. Halfway up the wall there was a score or so of nails festooned with loops of binder twine and she used these to anchor the greenery. Greg had stood and watched her for a while, anxious at the precarious way in which Gerry stretched sideways as she worked.

'You should move the ladder, Gerry. It's not a good idea to lean over like that. Better still, leave it for me to do, I'll be free in a little while.' Gerry had come slowly down the ladder and stood facing Greg. In her arms was a bundle of inky-berried ivy and Dorcas, suddenly aware, stopped to watch the cousins. Greg took the ivy from Gerry, tossing it on to a bale of straw and Dorcas quite expected to see him fold Gerry in his arms and kiss her. It was as if something which she had always known had become indisputably apparent to Dorcas and she found herself holding her breath, still and observant.

At last Gerry gave a little laugh. 'I've been up

ladders before you know, but thanks.' Dorcas heard Gerry's confident voice waver as she brushed past Greg to stand in the fresh air, her hands fumbling for a cigarette in the pocket of her corduroy trousers. Years of discipline prevented Gerry from smoking in the barn and Greg walked by her without a glance. Dorcas heard the tractor start up and rumble away until the sound became no more than a threat in the distance like a disturbed wasp in a rotten apple.

Dorcas felt shaken by what she had seen and so abruptly understood. She returned to her task of folding knives and forks into napkins, wondering if Lally knew about Gerry and Greg. She thought it improbable as Lally seemed to have no thought at the moment for anything other than that which directly concerned her.

Dorcas looked around for Lally but saw only Davy, patiently separating out ropes of fairy lights from an anguine tangle piled in a laundry basket at his feet. He caught Dorcas's eye and smiled at her but she didn't bother to acknowledge him except to call out, 'Do you know where Lally is, Davy? I haven't seen her for ages.'

'She's arranging the flowers and thought it would be easier to do it in the kitchen and then carry them across. If you want her for anything in particular, Dorcas, I could find her for you if you like; I wouldn't mind a break from this job as I don't seem to be getting anywhere.' Davy gave a gentle tug on the knotted wires. 'It's almost as if they are deliberately resisting any efforts to prise them apart, wouldn't you say?'

'You *are* talking about the fairy lights?'

'Of course — what else?' Davy's voice was ingenuous but Lally was almost sure that he was aware of the little scene that had just been played out between Greg and Gerry at the foot of the ladder. Dorcas also suspected that Davy, coming lately into the association of which she and Lally had so long been a part, saw very clearly the fallibility in each one of them which they ignored, used as they were to accepting what was offered openly as a family accepts decisions without necessarily approving of the actions of each individual member. If Davy had a drawback apart from his age, Dorcas thought, it was the slight hint of maliciousness which prompted him to allow his knowledge of situations to become apparent in such a way as to undermine another's confidence. It was a weakness in a character of otherwise exemplary probity, but in spite of the reliability and care for Lally which Davy displayed Dorcas was finding it difficult to warm to him.

Gerry, rather to Dorcas's annoyance, appeared to think that Davy was a good match for Lally and disagreed with Dorcas that he was cold and much too old. So often in the past the three girls had sat together on one bed and talked until sensible discussion had degenerated into laughter and nonsense but now Lally usually found an excuse to be busy elsewhere when Dorcas and Gerry wanted to talk.

The little bedroom over the kitchen no longer seemed to Lally to be a banishment. It had become a retreat, a haven from the inquisitive, and she was happy to be able to close the door and think in secret of the future she would so soon share with Eugene. There was no need for anyone other than Eugene and her to share this knowledge until he made the announcement of their engagement at the party but Lally knew that Davy must be made aware of the situation before then and on the second day after she and her parents had arrived at Petty Place Lally took him to the meadow under the ash trees where she had first decided that she must dedicate herself to saving Eugene. Lally had told Davy in the simplest of words that God had shown her the path that she must follow and how grateful she had been to Davy for his friendship which had allowed her to be free to fulfil her destiny by never making any physical demands on her.

Davy had laughed and said that he couldn't imagine that Eugene Jarvie would desist from making physical demands on her and was Lally prepared for that? Davy had tried sitting on the grass but, finding it too damp, he had stood up again and was looking down the hill to where two people were walking together close to the gorse hedge which even now glowed with golden flowers. They were deep in conversation and Davy recognised Gerry's red hair and guessed that her companion was Greg. In the short time he had been at Petty Place Davy had realised that an unusual situation existed between the cousins and that he seemed to be the only person who was aware of its implications.

Davy's determination to marry Lally was not diminished in the slightest by talk of her future being with Eugene and he refused to take seriously what she was trying to make him understand so that he should not be hurt when the time came to reveal that she and Eugene were going to be married. 'He sent for me you see, Davy, and I knew it was the sign that I'd been waiting for so I had to come. You're the only other person who knows but I thought it only fair to tell you as you've been such a good friend.'

'I'll always be a friend, Lally, and I'll still be here when you need me.' Lally had looked so beautiful, like a wood nymph, still and graceful under the ash trees and her curious, turquoise eyes had been lit with a joy that made Davy fearful. 'I'll always be here.' Davy thought of the shadowy figures he had seen, of the laughter overheard, and his heart ached for Lally. 'Perhaps it would be better if you didn't tell anyone else just yet, let it be our secret.'

'Not for long, Davy. Everyone'll know soon now but I think I should tell Dorcas, don't you?'

'No!' Davy spoke sharply but Lally, lost in her own euphoric world, chose to disregard him.

'I didn't know what to say to her, Gerry. It was awful and I felt such a coward but what *could* I say? There she was, absolutely *alight* with happiness and wanting to share her secret with me and I couldn't stop her.' Dorcas removed little wedges of cotton wool from between her toes, *Fire and Ice* with which she had painted her nails, dry enough not to smudge.

'You must have said something.'

'I just sort of made *um* and *ah* noises, trying not to say *anything*. Oh, I know I should have done but I just couldn't, and now she *still* believes that Eugene wants to marry her. Oh, Gerry, what can I do?'

'Well, for a start, think about it rationally. Surely you can't imagine Lally as a farmer's wife?'

'Trogging about in gum boots for nine months of the year and helping at calvings? No, I suppose not. No, of course not and, besides, Lally can't cook and you know how much Eugene eats. In fact, I don't suppose that for years and years she's so much as ironed a handkerchief if she hasn't wanted to do it. Effie's looked after her for so long that Lally probably imagines a fairy comes in overnight and waves a magic wand over everything, just like we used to believe when we were little.'

'But we soon learned not to believe in fairies and I don't think that Lally ever has really.'

'I hesitate even to suggest that Davy is a fairy,' Dorcas gave Gerry a look that said more than her words before she went on, 'but he seems rather to have taken over from Effie as Lally's guardian and retainer, don't you think? I wonder if he's in love with her because we both know that Lally's not a bit in love with him.'

'I think he is, in his own way.'

'And what way is that?'

'Not in the way you and Eugene are, that's for sure.'

'More a courtly love? A meeting of minds?'

Gerry shrugged. 'I'd say,' she paused, 'well, I can't imagine them *doing* very much. I don't mean just now, but *ever*. Lally needs someone to look after her and Davy's very good at that but I shouldn't imagine there's much fun involved in it all. Not,' she added with a sideways look at Dorcas, 'like you and my cousin in the hayloft.'

Dorcas laughed and unscrewed the top of the nail polish again. 'Do you think this colour's too bright? A bit tarty?'

'Yes. And yes. But does that worry you?'

'Not a bit.' Dorcas started to outline a half-moon on the little finger of her right hand. 'Perhaps if we just ignore it, it'll go away and Lally will realise herself that it's just not on – her and Eugene, I mean.'

Gerry looked around for an ashtray and finding none emptied hair grips and odd buttons out of a small pottery basket on Dorcas's dressing-table before flicking ash into it. She spoke cautiously. 'I don't think that's going to happen somehow. You know how odd Lally's been lately and I think this thing about Eugene is a sort of compulsion. She's absolutely convinced herself that he's mad for her.'

'He's not, is he? You know him better than me,

Gerry, so tell me the truth.' Dorcas had reached the thumb on her right hand and was admiring the effect of the bright red polish. She was so confident of Eugene's feelings for her that she was quite unprepared for Gerry's next words.

'The truth? The truth as I see it is that Eugene is very attracted to Lally, perhaps even a bit in love with her, but he knows that she won't do as a wife.' Gerry looked at Dorcas who was very still, concentrating on outlining a perfect half-moon. There was no change in Dorcas's expression but her face had flooded with colour and Gerry was afraid that she had said too much, but Dorcas had asked for the truth.

'And me?' Dorcas said quietly, 'Is he in love with me, Gerry, or is he just pretending? No, don't say anything, I don't want to know. But what I do know is that Lally's not going to get him and the sooner she realises that the better.'

'Dorcas, do be careful. Lally's so – what? Unbalanced? Whatever's always been wrong with her is worse now and this obsession with Eugene isn't rational. Sometimes I feel that she only needs a push and she'll go right over the edge.'

'She's got Davy, she can't have Eugene as well. Here.' Dorcas held out a piece of cotton wool and the nail polish remover to Gerry. 'Wipe this nail for me, will you? I've made a mess of it and I'll have to start again.'

'If Lally wants Eugene the fact that she has Davy isn't going to help. It doesn't. It doesn't help at all.' Gerry screwed the top back on the bottle of remover and handed it back to Dorcas who, alerted by the change in Gerry's voice, looked at her friend and saw that her hands were shaking as she lit another cigarette. 'Smoke,' said Gerry, 'gets in your eyes – as someone has already said.'

Dorcas put her arms around Gerry, fingers splayed so as not to undo the careful work of the last twenty minutes. 'Oh, Gerry, I'm so, so sorry but it'll work out all right, you'll see.'

'Not this time, Dorcas.' Someone walked along the corridor outside Dorcas's bedroom and the two girls waited but the footsteps passed on without hesitating and they heard the rattle of a key on the hotel's heavy key ring being fitted into a door further along the passage. 'Do you remember the day in the woods when I said that I'd tell you when I'd made up my mind what I was going to do with my life?' Dorcas nodded. 'Well, I have decided.'

'Tell me quickly!'

'Not now. Soon. Now we need to concentrate on you and Lally and Eugene.'

'"A pity beyond all telling is hid in the heart of love."'

'Let me guess. Shelley?'

'Yeats.'

'You don't do that nearly so much anymore you know. I quite miss your quotations although I hardly ever got them right but Eugene never reads anything except *Farmer's Weekly* and motoring magazines so you'll be wasting your time on him.'

'He's fetching us in the Austin to drive us to the party, did you know? At the moment he's polishing it and decorating it with ribbons and flowers and he intends to drive us all on to Home Farm before we start the dance. Isn't that sweet? I sometimes think he loves that car far more than any real person.' For a moment Dorcas looked smug as she knew that what she had just said wasn't true but she thought that it sounded adult and acceptably mature.

'It'll be a bit of a squash with us all in our long dresses but I suppose it *is* quite sweet. Have you seen Lally's dress? Effie hinted that it's something special even for her.'

'Probably virginal white – unlike ours.'

'If that's the only criterion yours should be scarlet and mine a murky pink.'

'Thanks.' Dorcas laughed and helped herself to one of Gerry's cigarettes, using the flat of her fingers so as to preserve the perfect finish on her nails. She inhaled once or twice but stopped suddenly, a hand to her throat. 'Oh, God, I'm going to be sick. Out of the way, Gerry.' Dorcas reached the wash-basin in the corner of her room just in time.

'I do hope,' Gerry said, 'that display is just nerves about tonight.'

'What else could it be? It can't be food poisoning

as I haven't eaten anything that we haven't all had. Oh! Oh, Gerry, you don't think . . . ?'

'I don't think anything.' Gerry looked at Dorcas for a long minute, too used to her mother's pregnancies to be in much doubt about the cause of Dorcas's sickness but too kind to voice her suspicions openly. At last she said, 'I'll turn the tables on you and give you a quotation. You don't have to guess who said it – actually in this case, who wrote it – but just think about it.'

'OK, I'm ready.'

'T.E.Lawrence.'

'Yes.'

'He wrote that he was re-reading *Lady Chatterley's Lover* with – and this is the important bit – "*with a slow deliberate carelessness*". Does that suggest anything to you?'

'It certainly wasn't slow nor really deliberate but I suppose, I'm sure really, that we've been careless and now . . . Oh well, it only speeds things up a bit and it is *thrilling* when you think about it. We've always said we'd like a *huge* family.'

'You don't mind?'

Dorcas had settled back on the corner of her bed, pale and rather upright, and now she looked at Gerry. 'Not a bit – and I'm sure Eugene won't either: I suppose I'd better go and find him to tell him the good news.' Dorcas smiled to herself, thinking of the woman she had met in the churchyard at her grandmother's funeral and whom she now knew to be the daughter of her grandfather's passing pleasure with a woman called Alice

Tancock; a half-Aunt whom Dorcas intended to get to know so that she would have someone near her in age when the older members of the family were gone. It amused her to think that she wasn't the first in her family to have disregarded the teachings of the chapel and she felt no regret nor remorse for the situation in which she now found herself.

'You don't think you should wait until you're sure? It might be a false alarm.'

Dorcas stood up, tall and heavy and, now, quite resolute, all frivolity suspended. 'Can't be, I'm as regular as clockwork and, in any case, what difference would it make? I told you that Lally isn't going to have Eugene and this is the one circumstance that even she can't argue with. No, this couldn't be better timing. Eugene'll be delighted, you wait and see but, Gerry, not a word, not a hint. Promise?'

'Of course.' Gerry gathered up her cigarettes and looked for her lighter, scrabbling among the folds of the creased counterpane on Dorcas's bed. 'I'm going to wash my hair now, give it time to dry before this evening.' She walked towards the door. 'Dorcas, whatever happens I'm right behind you, you know that, you and Eugene, and I'll try to smooth things over with Lally if I can but I think you should be prepared for a difficult time with her.'

'Oh it'll be all right. Dependable Davy will look after her: probably just what he wants actually, a lever to persuade her to succumb to his creepy, elderly charm.'

'Dorcas!'

'Don't be cross with me, Gerry, I'm not half as nice as you and never have been and I feel a bit sad that things are going to change because they'll never be *quite* the same once I'm married will they?'

Gerry said nothing but gave Dorcas a look which Dorcas seemed not to notice. She knew that it wasn't the fact that Dorcas would soon be a married woman that would change things, but the secret that Gerry had promised to share with Dorcas and with which she was still coming to terms herself. Gerry knew now with reassuring certainty that once she had left the art school she would enter the convent to teach drawing and painting in one of the schools run by the Order.

She knew she would have no choice as to where she was sent and hoped only that it would be a long way away: away from Greg and everything she understood to be forbidden to her for the rest of her life. Dorcas wouldn't understand, Gerry knew that, but Lally might. Lally might very well understand.

CHAPTER ELEVEN

Coral was wearing a two-piece of mauve brocade. It was an unhappy choice as the colour emphasised the pallor of her powder-enhanced complexion and quarrelled with the salmon-pink rouge and lipstick which she thought, mistakenly as anyone would have told her had she bothered to ask, would add glamour to her appearance. She had decided to leave off her support stockings for the evening although she knew that she would pay for it later and had, by willpower more than good sense, squeezed her feet into black patent leather pumps from a range for the wider foot.

A dark blue leather jewel case was open on the dressing-table, the current object of Coral's attention. She had sent Effie to find Lally and to bring her to the bedroom so that a suitable piece of jewellery might be given to Mary Marigold to wear with the dress that would make her the centre of attention at the party that evening.

Coral picked out a double string of pearls for herself and hesitated over a heavy Victorian locket and a row of amethyst beads, marred and made gaudy by each bead being separated from its neighbour by a gold spacer. Neither seemed quite right and Coral continued to look until she found a necklace of jet which she had restrung herself and which had a ragged and unattractive length of bare thread where she had inexpertly tied it off. This she put aside and rummaged some more until she found the pair of earrings she had in mind for Lally. The fact that they were made of black plastic that seemed to suggest that their provenance had been a Christmas cracker was immaterial to Coral; they almost matched the necklace and would do very well.

There was a light tap on the door and Lally came into the room. She was wearing a yellow dressing-gown, the colour softer than buttercup, brighter than primrose, that Effie had made for her. Lally had allowed her hair to grow and now, newly washed, it hung on to her shoulders, its startling colour still as pale as when she had been a child.

'I wonder why your hair never darkened like other people's?'

'What?' Lally was disconcerted by her mother's remark.

'Other blonde children have hair that gets darker as they get older; you notice it at the school gates. By the time they're ten or eleven they all seem to have lost that real fairness but you never have. I suppose you've just got to learn to live with it.' Coral patted the coils of hair on her neck that Effie and artifice contrived to keep as auburn as they had always been. 'Never mind, you can always have a rinse to tone it down a bit.'

'But I don't want to tone it down a bit. There's nothing wrong with my hair.' Lally could have added, *And when, I'd like to ask, did you ever stand at any school gates?* but thought better of it, knowing a scene would ensue if she challenged her mother too often, suspecting that this was Coral's intent.

As it was Coral's next remark was spoken in a voice heavy with patient endurance. 'If you say so, Mary Marigold, but a cut and a nice rinse would make all the difference.'

Silence settled on the three women. Lally, who had arrived in her mother's room full of anticipation of the happiness that would be confirmed to everyone that evening, now stood with clenched fists hidden in yellow silk folds and hated her mother. *No, of course I don't hate her. I never have, not really hated her and, anyway, soon now I shall be free. Free to go to Eugene and not be bullied any more or told that I'd be better looking with a rinse or what a pity I haven't a talent like Gerry. Soon, soon Eugene will make up for everything because he's chosen me. Not that immoral great Dorcas or any of the other girls who hang around him. He sent me a sign and I came and tonight everyone will share our happiness and everything will be all right from now on.*

'Lally!' Lally looked at Coral as if she hardly noticed her. 'Lally! What are you doing, just standing there with that silly smile on your face? Come here, I want to give you something.' Coral held out her hand and Lally went to stand by her, not touching her mother, waiting, unconcerned in her newly acquired equanimity.

Coral picked up the necklace and the terrible earrings and held them out to her daughter. 'These are for you to wear tonight with your dress.' Coral gave a smile that wasn't a smile at all. 'I shall expect to see them on you so don't think you can conveniently forget them.'

Effie suddenly started to sing a tune that neither mother nor daughter recognised and almost snatched the beads from Coral's hand. As she slipped them over Lally's head, concealing the frayed string under her hair, Effie managed to whisper, 'We'll lose them later on,' without a break in the frenzy of her song.

Lally glanced over her shoulder at Mary Marigold reflected in the glass on the dressing-table but made no comment. She heard her mother say, 'That looks lovely, really classy. You can't beat the genuine article.' Lally slipped the earrings into the pocket of the yellow dressing-gown and smiled at Coral. She could afford to be generous this one last time, but not so generous that she would even contemplate wearing either the disagreeable necklace nor its unpleasant plastic satellites. Coral seemed satisfied and patted the side of the bed. 'Come and sit down and talk to me. We haven't had a girlie talk for a long time and I miss my Mary Marigold now that she's growing up and in such demand with the boys.'

'Oh, Mummy, it's only Davy and he's hardly a boy. Besides, he's as much your friend as mine.' *Careful, careful, Lally, don't give even a hint about Eugene. You can't afford for anything to go wrong now. Not that anything will, but Coral might let the secret out and spoil the surprise.*

'Have you seen the dresses that Gerry and Dorcas are wearing?' Coral had put her cold fingers over Lally's and Lally made an effort not to move her hand away. 'They won't be anything like yours, of course, but I dare say they'll be nice enough and, after all, they wouldn't even try to compete.'

'Why should they want to? It's a birthday party not a heat in the Miss Great Britain competition.' Effie sniggered before snuffing out the noise in further song.

Lally was desperate to leave the claustrophobia of Coral's bedroom. It was a room more suited to the word *boudoir* and it was not the location but something about Coral herself to which attached faint memories of stale fruit, the cloying smell of unwashed powder puffs, armpits and Devon Violets sucked to sweeten the breath. Coral's satin and lace underwear belonged to a time of hand washing and careful ironing; her travelling cases too heavy for a woman alone to carry. Coral brought herself complete into the life of everyone she visited, making no allowance for other domestic arrangements and using Effie as her go-between, the simple child no-one would refuse.

Now Lally looked at her mother and knew that the hour of her deliverance was near. Eugene had never cared about Coral's moods and laughed at her, pretending to mistake spite for humour, malice for wit if, indeed, he thought about it at all. He had no need to fear her and Lally knew that under Eugene's protection she would at last be safe from the incursions made by Coral for no more reason than that she was bored.

'I ought to go,' Lally said, standing up. 'Will you come and help me do up my dress, Effie? In about half an hour?'

'You can't go yet.' Coral's voice, used so often as a restraint to delay or detain Lally now sounded no more than a plaintive whisper and Lally hardly hesitated in her walk to the door.

Dorcas had seemed almost relieved when Lally had said that she would prefer to dress in her own room, pretending to accept Lally's assurance that there would be less of a crush that way. Lally had bathed and now sat at the little table that held her few cosmetics and her hairbrush and her aquamarine earrings. She knew exactly how Dorcas and Gerry would giggle over shared eye shadow, exclaiming with extravagant annoyance as they caught a nylon stocking with the rough edge of a thumb nail. She saw in her mind's eye Dorcas's plump shoulders leaning forward as Gerry did up the row of hooks and eyes on the substantial brassière that Dorcas needed to contain the soft flesh around her waist, and how Gerry would brush her hair without once looking in the glass before tossing her head from side to side so that all the careful neatness would be disarranged once more.

Lally knew that they would talk about her; how bold she was becoming, how assured, and wonder together about the reason for the change in her. They would discuss her dress as they scrambled into their own, tugging and shifting a bodice, turning to make a skirt flare as they moved. Lally had seen what Dorcas and Gerry were to wear but her own frock had been kept in Coral's bedroom until Effie had moved it covertly to Lally's own room, where it now hung from the open door of the wardrobe.

Lally rolled on the stockings that Effie had laid out for her and stepped into a silk half-petticoat, shivering as she thought of Eugene's eyes watching her as she put on her clothes every day; his eyes sliding over her slender arms, lingering on her tender winged shoulders. Lally made herself stop there, aware that she was in danger of harbouring impure thoughts. She remembered Mother Mary John's advice to find a suitable distraction and forced herself to count the strokes as she brushed her hair. Some electricity in the air or generated by her own body charged through every strand and as she watched it rose in an uncontrollable white halo, springing upwards from the brush.

When Effie slipped into the room she stopped,

startled into silence, by the sight of Lally's pale hair, an aureole around her head. 'Well, whatever are we going to do with *that* then?'

Lally laughed and in the shadows far back in the room Eugene laughed too. 'It'll settle down in a bit. Let me put my dress on and then you can try to do something with my hair.'

Gerry shook her head from side to side just as Lally had imagined her doing. Dorcas, watching her with concern, thought how muted her hair looked, the colour less vivid than she remembered. Dorcas had been concerned to see how thin Gerry had become, her strong athletic body now hinting at a slightness that was quite unexpected. Had she, Dorcas wondered, ignored Gerry's needs, too involved with herself, with Eugene, with their growing mutual fascination?

Gerry had made a joke as she became aware of Dorcas studying her as they stood together in their underwear before putting on their make-up and insinuating themselves last of all into their dresses. Dorcas, round cheeks as firm as apples, was not deceived and saw clearly for the first time that her friend had moved away to a place where she could not follow. In years to come when Dorcas, the mother of five children, remembered her perceived neglect of Gerry she would stem her impatience with the trivialities of her children's little lives and listen to them with hard-won patience. She watched them too, and heard everything that they did not say in the spaces between their words. But now, excited and full of anticipation, the two girls shared Crème Puff and with their little fingers stroked Vaseline along their eyebrows to make them shine.

'That's it then.' Gerry looked at herself in the glass, making a little pout before blotting her lipstick on an old red handkerchief which Dorcas had taken from her mother's drawer. Dorcas slid on to the stool next to her and Gerry moved over to make room for them both. They sat silently looking at themselves, at each other, at two small girls who had forged an unlikely friendship which would leave behind memories of long, wet afternoons and forbidden games: of forgiven betrayals, unbreakable secrets and rude, unremembered jokes.

'That's it then,' Gerry said again and Dorcas murmured, *"Friendships begin with liking or gratitude".'*

'Go on then, enlighten me: I'm resigned.'

'Mrs Gaskell. And it's true isn't it? Years and years ago you lent me your cardigan at one of Lally's ghastly birthday parties and I've been grateful to you ever since.'

'Don't be so silly, Dorcas, we just like each other, that's all, but while we're on the subject, I'm grateful to you too, you know.'

'Whatever for?'

'For being so discreet about me and Greg; never asking any questions.' Gerry looked at her pale, freckled hands. 'I don't think anyone else even guesses ...'

'. . . I think that Davy does.'

'Oh.' Gerry was quiet for a moment or two. 'Well, perhaps you can keep a lid on it, pretend he's made a mistake. If he ever says anything that is.'

'I'll blackmail him – and enjoy doing it.'

'Could you? He seems utterly blameless to me. Ominously so.'

'Oh, I'll find something. There's always something. But, Gerry, about Greg . . .'

'Not now, Dorcas.' Gerry stopped and then said more gently, 'Sorry, didn't mean to bite your fingers off but there really isn't anything to say. It was all over before it ever really started. Just not on, us being first cousins and good Catholics. He's going to leave the farm, you know, and he'll soon find someone else.'

'And you?'

'Ah.' Gerry managed a laugh which almost convinced Dorcas that it was genuine. 'In a way I've already found someone else but let's change the subject. Race you into the frocks.'

'I wonder what Lally's is like and what Aunt Coral has managed to do to undermine her and totally spoil the evening for her.'

'She really is quite, quite awful isn't she? Just *imagine* growing up with a mother like that. No wonder Lally's so odd, although I do think that Davy is a sort of buffer between them.'

'A sort of buffer is right – a real, old-fashioned buffer of the dreariest kind.'

'You're wrong, Dorcas. I know you don't like him much but there's a lot more to Davy than you give him credit for. Mum says he did undercover work during the war and was decorated several times but he never talks about it.'

'You're right there, I don't much like him but I think it's because I want Lally to have something more than just another keeper. She should have *fun* and wickedness and excitement.'

'Hay lofts and sunwarm grass?'

'That would be a start, instead of dinners in the kind of hotels where her parents go to eat and drives in the country as if she's the inmate of a retirement home being taken for an outing.'

'Oh, Dorcas, you can't choose for her. Can you even *imagine* Lally with her hair full of straw and grass stains on her knickers?'

Dorcas pretended to consider this suggestion for a moment. 'Lally, no – Mary Marigold, perhaps.'

'Aren't they the same person?'

'Oh no. I think,' Dorcas said slowly, 'that Mary Marigold might well enjoy wickedness and excitement in large measures but Lally accepts the protection of someone who will never know Mary Marigold. That way she doesn't have to face the unacceptable fact that she has become what her mother has made her.'

There were pools of light in the room, only slightly hindered by curtains of voile which Dorcas had pulled back so that she and Gerry might see themselves more clearly. Her bedroom overlooked a courtyard and she seldom drew the heavier linen curtains, oblivious to the need. Bars of late sunshine painted the candlewick counterpane, highlighting the bald patches where a younger Dorcas had pulled out tuft after tuft of the soft cotton whenever she could think of nothing better to do. Over the years it had become a map of measles and a broken leg, the boredom of sore throats and, one bad winter, a bout of flu that had lingered and left her feeling weepy and out of sorts until Gerry had come to Home Farm for Easter and had taken over Dorcas's recuperation. It was during that holiday that Dorcas had first become aware of Eugene as a figure separate from his brothers and not just as one of Gerry's cousins.

Dorcas, used to solitude, preferring to take an increasingly important role in the kitchens of Petty Place than to mingling with the guests at the hotel, had thought long and deeply about her friendship with Lally and in the hours she spent alone Dorcas had come to understand that there was nothing she could do to rescue her.

'Dorcas?' Gerry touched her friend's arm. 'Don't let's be gloomy. This is such a special evening for all of us, forget Davy the Dull and concentrate on you and Eugene – oh, I'm so glad you'll be marrying into the family – and seeing that Lally enjoys herself and that Coral is kept miles away from her. Actually I've told Aidan that it's his duty to look after Coral – be good practice for him for when he's a parish priest and has to be nice to all the dotty old ladies who've got a pash on him.'

'On with the motley then?' Dorcas let the heavy tartan taffeta slide down her raised arms and turned to Gerry who tried to move the zip up its plastic teeth. 'Deep breath, old thing, and hold it.' Gerry laughed, 'You bought this a while ago remember.'

'Oh, Gerry, I'm not showing already am I?'

'Not to the undiscerning eye, but it *is* a bit tight round the waist. Not to worry though, you look absolutely super. Glowing.'

'Not radiant? Isn't that how mothers-to-be are supposed to look?'

'Actually I think radiant is for brides. Blooming is for mums. Come on, do me up.'

If Dorcas's blue-and-green tartan was tight, Gerry's burnt orange corded silk had room to spare but Dorcas said nothing, adjusting the halter neck to cover as much as possible of Gerry's newly bony shoulders. The freckles on her pale skin stood out like a sprinkling of tiny autumn leaves and Gerry made a face. 'Wrong colour, isn't it? Shall I change into something else? My old blue?'

'Don't you dare. You look lovely, Gerry, but you always do and your hair is so beautiful, like new pennies.' The sentiment behind the words was true but Gerry wished that she looked as she had a year ago so that Greg would remember her as she had been when they had only played at being in love. Now Dorcas and Gerry, knowing that they would never again share such carefree familiarity, gave a last look at themselves in the glass and went together down the front staircase, two pairs of specially dyed satin shoes stepping out in unison to meet Lally and whatever the evening would bring.

Warmth, light and music filled the transformed barn, embracing and drawing into intimacy everyone who passed under the arch of rainbow-coloured lights that Davy had so diligently separated, tested and finally arranged over the cart-sized double doors. If there were cobwebs and dust they were invisible, lost in the dusky shadows that waited, unassailable, outside the circle of colour and brilliance to creep back, to draw softly once more a mantle over two hundred years of secrecy.

In the middle of a circle of young people who stood together near the doorway was Lally. Davy was not part of the group but lingered close by and he watched Lally as if waiting to deflect the hurt which he knew was coming and of which he had tried to warn her. Lally was luminous with joy.

Her dress was everything that Coral had worked for. Gone were the layers of organdie, the drifts of tulle: Lally stood dressed in a column of satin the colour of old ice found in the depths of a glacier, a bell-shaped skirt seeming more fluid than material as it swayed with every movement from her tiny waist, and with every movement sparkles and points of light were reflected from a bodice covered in silver embroidery with a pearl or a diamanté outlined by each ingenuous curve. Lally wore no jewellery apart from her aquamarine earrings, and her hair, her astonishing pale hair, was like frost on the ice of her dress. Her shoes had been made of the same embroidered material as the bodice of her dress and Dorcas noticed for the first time how tiny Lally's feet were. She was like a child wearing shoes she had found discarded in a trunk and seized upon so that she could dress up and pretend for a while to be almost grown up. Looking at Lally's sparkling little slippers Dorcas truly understood, far too late, that Lally was not like other people; it was the poignancy of those childish feet masquerading as an adult's that filled Dorcas with foreboding as the knowledge of what she was about to do became clear to her.

The three girls danced with Eugene and Aidan, with Greg and Davy: they danced with Vernon and with Billy Bassett and even with each other, improvising with their arms linked to the sound of a zither playing the Harry Lime theme. When supper was announced they looked around for their accepted escorts and Davy and Eugene moved towards Dorcas and Lally but it was Aidan who claimed Gerry. She gave every appearance of pleasure at being with him and at the same time seemed unaware that Greg, more than slightly drunk, had his arm around the shoulders of a girl known to the Jarvie family as The Cultured Pearl.

Pearl Makepiece had one of those curious voices

whose pitch or tone, although not coarse or particularly loud, seemed to flow over and engulf any intervening noise and arrive, undiminished, at some distant listener's ear. Now Gerry was aware of her giggling and calling to Greg as if he were a dog to be brought to heel. Gerry turned away quickly, glad that Aidan understood with no need for further explanation why she had abdicated her position as Greg's natural partner. She had forgotten how good a listener Aidan had always been and she was grateful for the time he had taken with her before offering his services as an alternative escort for the evening.

At a table which stood a little apart from the others Lally had noticed the card with her name on it placed between Davy and Aidan. She knew it to be a mistake so she removed the card with DORCAS on it from Eugene's right-hand side and substituted for it the one that said LALLY. Satisfied, Lally sat down and waited for Davy to bring her a plate of food. Dorcas and Gerry arrived at the table together and exchanged conspiratorial glances when they saw where Lally was sitting. Gerry said nothing but Dorcas picked up three of the cards and rearranged them so that she was once more on Eugene's right and Lally was back between Davy and Aidan. 'Must have got muddled up,' she said cheerfully. 'I should have done it myself instead of leaving it to Aidan; he hasn't a clue, unworldly as he is.'

Gerry was watching Lally as Dorcas spoke and for a moment, deep in those strange, pale eyes, she saw something that made her shiver but almost at once Davy appeared and placed in front of Lally a plate arranged to conceal how little it actually contained. Lally smiled her thanks and taking up a fork pretended to eat. Dorcas made no pretence of her enjoyment of the food and Lally thought how indecorous she looked, face shining from the exertions of the Gay Gordons, her mouth full of cold roast beef, of which much more crowded her plate.

Lally, picking at lettuce and a potato salad, thought of the close call Eugene had had in escaping a life with Dorcas, who even now in her flattering tartan taffeta dress, hinted at the figure she would develop in middle age. Lally had tried to win Eugene's attention but only once had he smiled directly at her and asked in the voice which Lally thought of as the one he used in public how she was enjoying herself. She had replied in a way that puzzled him.

'I know it must be hard for you to keep the secret, Eugene darling, but I haven't told *anyone* so that the surprise won't be spoiled before you make the announcement later on. I want to be able to see *all* their faces when you do.' Eugene had smiled more warmly at Lally, amused that although she always refused to touch alcohol she must, inadvertently, have had a little too much to drink. He suspected Greg and the fruit punch.

He was surprised though that Lally seemed to be acquainted with such exactitude about the timing of the announcement of his engagement to Dorcas but he only managed to say, 'Thanks, Lally, I appreciate that,' before there had been a tap on his shoulder and Lally had slipped into Davy's arms to finish the dance. Davy could see her every heartbeat in a vein in Lally's neck and he wanted to take her away, to shield her, but had to watch hopelessly as he witnessed the constant rhythm of her heart's desire for someone else.

The cake was cut, the speeches made and Lally, in a fever of excitement, sat looking as cool and calm as if unaware that something unusual was about to happen. Only Davy, sitting beside her, saw that her fingers were so tightly clasped together that they looked bloodless, as white and numb as a marble angel's on a grave. Davy wanted to reach out and touch her but Lally, as if anticipating his thoughts, turned briefly towards him and Davy saw the look in her eyes that had so disturbed Gerry not long before.

Eugene got to his feet. *Now, now, Eugene. Tell them that you love me and that you have chosen me above all others to share your life; to be your wife and your lover. Your lover: oh yes, I'm ready now to make the sacrifice. I've held your love in my heart for so long to keep you pure but now there won't be any more sin, only love and you and me. For ever and ever. Amen.* '... although I did ask her father's permission and he seemed surprisingly anxious for me to take her off his hands.' There was laughter as Eugene looked towards the table where Coral and Billy sat with Alma and Vernon. Eugene went on, 'And I'm therefore delighted to be able to share our happiness with all of you, our closest friends.'

Lally clutched the seat of her chair, ready to stand up and take her place beside Eugene, to accept the congratulations of everyone who had always dismissed her as no more than the dutiful daughter of an invalid mother, fit only to teach shorthand and typing to girls who would mock her principles and speculate about her proclivities.

Eugene turned to his right. *Now, Eugene, is it now?* 'I give you the future Mrs Eugene Jarvie – Miss Dorcas Westley.'

Lally was on her feet but Eugene had his arm around Dorcas, a crowd surrounding them, smiling and holding raised glasses. 'Why is Eugene kissing Dorcas? I don't understand. He's going to marry me so why is he kissing Dorcas like that? She's a sinner you know and I've been keeping Eugene pure for years – keeping him away from trollops like her.' Lally seemed to be talking very loudly to herself and Davy put his arms around her. Aidan, observant and the only one of the three brothers still to be entirely sober, moved quickly to help him. 'Take her into the house,' he said, 'and I'll stay with her. Did you know about this?' Davy nodded and together the two men half carried Lally towards the farmhouse.

In the warmth of the kitchen Aidan helped Lally to the chair beside the Rayburn where his father usually sat. 'He sent for me you know, a secret message but I understood it and I came to him. What I don't understand is how a slut like Dorcas made him say the wrong words. I suppose, though, that once she'd made him say them he was too decent – because he *is* decent, you know that Aidan, whatever other people may say – he was too decent to admit his mistake and he had to pretend to be going to marry Dorcas. I'll sort it out. You must take me back to the barn: I must go back to Eugene.' Lally struggled, agitated and beginning to shout.

Even in his anxiety to calm Lally Davy was surprised to hear her using language of which he had thought her incapable, words that shocked exploding from her, but too clearly enunciated for there to be any mistake of her intention. The torrent of abuse and disbelief ended abruptly as Lally began to laugh, shrill cackles that raised the hairs on the back of Davy's neck. Almost at once the laughter became eclipsed by terrible tears.

'I'll fetch Effie.' Aidan, almost forgotten, spoke from the shadows of the half-lit kitchen.

'I'll go,' Davy said. 'I'll collect Lally's things and see if I can find Dr Durham, he's in there somewhere.' Davy looked at Lally and saw, not the beautiful, fragile girl of an hour ago, but a tiny, hunched figure whose hands were claws and whose face seemed to have collapsed like paper in the rain. 'Watch her, Aidan, I won't be long.'

Aidan, kneeling by Lally's chair, looked so like Eugene that Lally began once more to understand that all that had happened was an illusion, a trial to test her love and through which she had come triumphant, or why was Eugene here with her, alone in his house when Dorcas was still in the barn?

Lally put her arms around Aidan's neck. 'Your Lally's here and I've saved you from that whore, Dorcas. Now you can have your reward – you can kiss me. But nothing more, not until we're married.' Lally's attempt to be playful was horrible to see and Aidan unclasped her arms and stood up.

'I'm Aidan, Lally, not Eugene. Remember?'

'Are you sure? You look just like Eugene.' Lally was doubtful.

'Yes I do, but I'm quite sure: I'm the one who's going to be a priest and Eugene is a farmer.'

'I'm thirsty, Aidan-the-priest, can I have a drink?' Lally sounded pathetic, a poorly child, and Aidan went towards the cupboard to fetch a glass. The kitchen had been left for the evening with only one low light on and he disappeared for a moment into the rim of darkness that surrounded the central brighter spot. It was long enough and when he turned around with a tumbler in his hand Lally had gone.

'Jesus, Mary and Joseph,' Aidan said, an expression he had never used before, dredged from his subconscious where it had lain since last heard spoken by an Irish girl who had helped his mother with the three boys when Aidan was ten. 'Dear God, help me.' He hesitated for a moment, unsure whether to check first along the passage that led to the lavatory or to go outside and look for signs that Lally had slipped back to the barn.

The decision was never made as the back door swung open of its own accord and Effie, followed by Davy carrying Lally's stole and glittery little evening bag, came through it, startled to find the door already open. One look at Aidan's face told Davy what he feared but before either man could speak they heard the cough and gentle splutter of the Austin which had been parked near the house when Eugene had brought the three girls over from Petty Place.

Afterwards Aidan could remember stretching out his hand towards the table in the middle of the kitchen to place the glass there in safety but in the realisation of what the noise outside meant the glass rolled to the edge of the table and fell, smashing itself to smithereens on the red-tiled floor, where it lay, overlooked, until someone noticed it and swept it up the next day.

Outside the house, in that part of its surroundings which was neither farm nor garden, Davy stood and watched a thin emission of smoke coming from the exhaust pipe of Eugene's car as Lally drove it out of the yard. He thrust the ice-coloured wrap and the beaded bag into Effie's arms and ran towards his own car, fumbling for the ignition keys as he went.

It was a beautiful night, an almost full moon painting a silver pathway down the middle of the road, lighting the way along which Lally drove. The music from the party was muted, filtered through a hedge as thick and as old as the house and as the lights became less obtrusive Davy saw that Lally had not bothered to turn on the Austin's headlights in her frenzy to escape.

Aidan had followed Davy, wrenching open the passenger door and throwing himself into the seat of the already moving car. Without taking his eyes off the Austin Aidan said softly, 'I don't think she can drive you know.' Davy said nothing, accelerating, intent on overtaking Lally before the road curved sharply to the right as it approached the bridge spanning the river. It was the same river which rose in the hills behind the farm, meandering and growing wider until it fed the water meadows where the ash trees grew on the bank, the mysterious place where everyone saw a vision of what they wanted to see and where Lally had dedicated her life to saving Eugene.

Aidan looked towards Davy again and understood that what lay beneath the dry, pedantic manner was a man made old too soon by war who saw once more the destruction of all that he most loved and had never thought to find again.

They were too late, of course. Lally steered erratically and faster than the Austin had ever managed before, down the moonlit pathway which ended on the first granite pillar of the bridge, slanted sideways and then continued in its brilliance over the dark, secret water of the river to the further bank.

It was the noise, the first impact, the clatter and tinkle of metal and glass, the rustle of running-boards and radiator and headlamps settling in pieces on the ground: it was the hiss of steam like some small, stalled train escaping into the velvety night air that stayed in the memory for ever. Lally had been thrown clear of the wheels which were still spinning when Davy, slowly because there was no need of haste, stopped his own car and knelt beside her on the silent, silver grass.

Davy was hardly aware of Aidan or the gentle slurring of his words of the prayers for the dying. When the soft Latin mumble penetrated Davy's consciousness he turned towards the younger man. 'Go back to the house, Aidan, ring for an ambulance and bring Bruce Durham back with you. And stop those damned prayers – she isn't dead. Hurry. Hurry.'

Aidan took another look at Lally's injured body and tried to remember how her face had been without the interlacing wounds that were beginning to bleed, pearls of blood issuing from every gash and laceration as they dribbled and ran into the folds of Davy's jacket.

'Go on, man.' Aidan pulled a rug from the back seat of Davy's car and placed it near Lally before trying to turn the key in the ignition with fingers that shook. He steadied his right hand with his left and backed the car carefully around the wreck of the Austin and the girl whose dress caught and retained the radiance of the moonlight and whose burning white hair was dark with blood. She lay in Davy's arms on the gravelly grass until Lally, whom he had loved, merged into one with Mary Marigold, whom he had never known, and both became part of the night.

CHAPTER TWELVE

Violet scrabbled all the old photographs together, any thought of sorting them forgotten, when Dorcas suggested a walk to the stables now that the rain had stopped. The air was fresh, almost cold, and the late winter sun gleamed on the river, turning it into a ribbon of silver gauze. The bridge was still called the 'new' bridge although it was a long time since it had been built to replace the old one of stone that had stood there before and around which memories lingered long after the skid marks and broken glass had been cleared from the drive.

Violet, as talkative and bright as Dorcas was silent, was happy to be out alone with her mother. It was seldom that any of the children had Dorcas's uninterrupted attention all to themselves and Violet was determined to make the most of it. She seemed oblivious to Dorcas's withdrawal.

Dorcas had recently begun to allow herself to think about Lally, to feel the sadness and regret for her short life that she had buried beneath layers of busyness, of children's activities, of Eugene's demands. It was as if Lally's death were the catalyst which had altered the lives of everyone around her; as if that one small, disregarded person, by leaving too early, allowed spaces to close which were not yet ready for securing and forced decisions on those who were not altogether yet free to make them.

To Billy and Coral their daughter's death exaggerated their individual feelings towards her, so that Billy seemed to add Lally's years to his own and he grew older as if he were carrying Lally's age, exponentially added to his own. Coral, who saw her investment in the future dispersed just as it was coming to fruition and in whose extravagant grief neither Alma nor Dorcas truly believed, put on a show as the bereft mother which outshone any of her previous performances but only Effie knew for certain that the tears and pitiful silences were replaced in private by enhanced viciousness, conducted now more secretly than ever and centred on Effie alone. But Effie didn't count, she never had.

When Coral died and Billy married Teresa Driscoll as Coral had predicted, Effie's job at the house in Advent Gardens came to an end so she gathered together the little mementoes she had taken from Lally's room, the jackdaw hoard which over the years Lally had acquired and which Effie had hidden in her own chocolate box of treasures so that there would be no recriminations should Lally be found in possession of things over which she had no title. There was a tiny pottery cat and cufflinks, odd sparkly earrings and a pink perspex bracelet which Effie recognised as one that Coral had given her for Christmas long ago: combs, propelling pencils — a number of these — a beaded purse, a penknife. They filled the box and into any spaces in between there were wedged tiny chairs and a coal scuttle and gold-framed pictures that Dorcas had missed from her crate-and-wallpaper doll's house over the years. These Effie retrieved and hid carefully in cotton wool in a cigar box, pretending to Dorcas when she returned them that they had turned up unexpectedly in a sideboard drawer when Billy and Teresa had been sorting out furniture to send to the auction. Dorcas was not deceived.

Effie had never worried about where she would go when Billy sold the house in Advent Gardens for hadn't Vernon Orme offered her a job at Petty Place any time she wanted it? She wanted it now and settled happily into the room over the kitchen where Lally had sometimes stayed when the house was full. Effie's few belongings seemed to fill the small space; she felt at home there, secure and snug surrounded by memories of Lally. Effie even enjoyed the noise which drifted upwards enclosing her in its casual companionship and she told Lally about it when she came to visit her at night. Not every night, Effie didn't expect that, but sometimes when the moon was full, painting a silver pathway on the road, Lally would come walking lightly over the grass, leaving no footprints and as young and beautiful as she had always been. She was sure of herself at last and happy in the way that Effie had always wanted her to be.

Effie kept these meetings secret but the next day she was always cheerful and full of song. Some of the young people who worked in the kitchen, noticing how Effie's mood seemed affected by the moon, pretended that she was a werewolf but Effie didn't mind. As long as Lally still came to her Effie didn't mind anything and did all the jobs that no-one else could be bothered with, becoming an indispensable and irrelevant member of Alma and Vernon's family.

Alma had argued against having Effie to live with them but Vernon had insisted that he had to honour his word to her and Alma had given in, amused at the way in which Effie became attached to Vernon, standing and watching him through her thick-lensed spectacles, humming softly to herself, ready to anticipate his need for a cup of tea, an ironed shirt, a change of shoes.

Alma understood Effie's devotion to Vernon for she herself had quickly learned that he was a man of principle, a kind and generous husband whose predictability was balanced by the absolute reliability of his word. He had given Alma everything she had ever wanted except more children and if their intimate life together was a little lacking in excitement Alma reminded herself of his goodness to her and accepted pragmatically that no-one had everything they wanted, accepting that she had more than most. If she was ever tempted to bring some of that excitement into her life, and there were plenty of approaches made by men staying on their own at Petty Place who were attracted by the plump, well-dressed wife of the owner of the hotel, she declined their propositions with oblique expressions of regret. Alma was friendly to all their visitors but familiar with none and had mourned for Lally, the child who had never grown up, as if she had been one of the babies that Alma had so longed for and had been denied.

In time Alma became a devoted grandmother to Dorcas and Eugene's children, wondering at the unusual and old-fashioned names they chose for them and worrying that Dorcas would be so circumscribed by maternity that she would become oblivious to Eugene. As Edmund was followed swiftly by Martha and Violet and, after a little pause about which Dorcas never spoke, by Swithin and Ottilie, the couple who had been so young when they married, seemed to settle and quite suddenly become middle aged, Dorcas growing into her face and figure as Alma had always assured her that she would.

When their family grew too large to be comfortable in the lodge where they had started their married life, the older Jarvies had suggested that they exchange homes with Dorcas and Eugene and together with four children they had moved into Home Farm a month before Ottilie was born.

Eugene and Dorcas seldom talked together about

Lally, neither to mention her name nor the circumstances of her death. It was as if to speak of her at all would allow the careful contrivance of the normality of their life together to crumble, to be torn away to expose what lay at the heart of their marriage, the memory that Eugene had accepted Lally's love for him with an arrogance that both he and Dorcas understood to have been partly responsible for her death. If Eugene had ever loved Lally it had been only infatuation he told himself, the teasing love of a young man intent on pleasure in those golden, sunlit days when Lally was a challenge and Dorcas so willing and familiar.

As long as it was never spoken of it could be ignored but the suppression of truth became habitual and Dorcas and Eugene remained united mainly by their children. It was when the last of the children left home that they realised with a terrible certainty that they had little left in common.

Although the knowledge of what had happened so long ago was never quite forgotten their dependence on each other had grown familiar and established and neither Dorcas nor Eugene would break that continuity. They were, moreover, very fond of one another and continued to live together contentedly enough, always faintly aware that something was missing. They became, in time, almost what they appeared to be.

No-one but Davy ever realised that between them lay a shadow, now nothing more than an image on a fading photograph in a shoe box, and when Eugene spoke of his first and favourite car, if anyone heard the regret in his voice they believed it to be for an Austin 10 not a girl who had died in the arms of Sir David Hosegood, the military historian, whose latest series on television was watched by everyone without fail on Sunday nights.

Davy had remained their greatest friend, godfather to Swithin and an adopted uncle to all the Jarvie children. Sometimes, after a good dinner, when Eugene walked around the yard last thing at night, Davy would turn to Dorcas and raise his glass and together they would drink a silent toast. He never married but emerged, almost overnight it seemed, into a character that everyone who watched him on television believed they knew – the man who brought the history of warfare alive for the man in the street. Davy, so gallant himself, so secretive, so dull, became loved by millions of people he never knew when all he had longed for was to be loved by one.

When Dorcas and Eugene had been married for twenty years Davy gave them a print of a picture called *Midsummer, East Fife*. 'It has always reminded me of the meadows under the ash trees,' he said. 'Somewhere where we all thought we'd seen what we most wanted.' He looked at Dorcas. 'Tell me what you see.'

Dorcas studied the painting. 'Cows in a river. A mixed herd, not all Friesians like we have here now. Very curious conical stooks of hay being loaded into a cart by three men – brothers, perhaps?' She looked at Davy, beginning to understand. 'Three houses; no, four, but only two painted in detail although even those are both half hidden by trees.'

'You're doing well. Go on.'

'Is this how you make your students learn?' Dorcas smiled at Davy and returned to the painting. 'On the right-hand side, on the slope where we used to sit, is some sort of encampment. There's a funny sort of tent like a tunnel and several figures, all women I think, gathered around a fire with babies and children – can't quite see how many.'

'Anything else?'

'Fields, trees, and the sea, of course. It looks calm and hazy like on a hot day. Shadows.'

'Look between the big trees,' Davy said gently, 'what do you see between the trees?'

Dorcas put out a hand for her reading glasses, a recent inevitability and looked more closely at the scene in front of her. 'A figure,' she said at last. 'Oh, Davy, there's a figure there. I didn't see it at first. A child.' She touched the moss-covered trunk and looked again. The small figure, almost hidden by the two great trees, was still there, joyous and free in the sunshine that dappled the grass under the ash trees by the river.

Violet, holding fast to Dorcas's hand, walked along the path by the river made slick and slippery by the rain. 'I was thinking about you and your friends in that old photo,' she said. 'I know about Gerry, of course, and

I suppose if you've been a nun for so long and then decide to jump ship you're entitled to be a *bit* dotty, but I've never heard you mention anyone called Lally. What happened to her?'

'Oh,' Dorcas said as they reached the new bridge, 'Lally's around somewhere I imagine. It's just that I don't see her any more.' She looked at the child by her side and smiled. 'Some friendships last for ever you see but some just seem to come to a natural end.' She swung her daughter's hand in its Fair Isle mitten high in the air. 'Come on, crumpets for tea.'

The Topiary Garden

JILL ROE

Lana Gifford has always been an admirable woman: a dutiful daughter, supportive wife (now a widow) and reliable and steadfast friend to Nell, Denise and Olive, colourful characters whom she meets once a week, working at the local charity shop.

But beneath the surface, Lana has a secret and the need to conceal this secret has always influenced her actions. As she watches her friends and their families go about their lives, finding happiness through various means, she decides the time is right for her, too, and she resolves to pursue her friendship with Marius Huysens, a Dutchman with a waterside garden full of trees and old roses, But will marrying Marius really make Lana happy or can she face the truth: that, ultimately, she will never be satisfied with what she has?

Praise for Jill Roe:

'A novel of great and civilised sensibility, and a real pleasure to read'

Fay Weldon in *The Mail on Sunday*

'Elegant, heartwarming comedy, shot through with sly humour'

Daily Telegraph

'A touching, bittersweet story'

Woman & Home

'A sensitive page-turner . . . clever and quietly compelling'
BBC Homes &Antiques

Jill Roe was the winner of a writing competition run by the *Mail on Sunday* and this encouraged her to start writing seriously. Born in West Cornwall, she now lives in Somerset with her husband. Her previous novels, *Angels Flying Slowly*, *A New Leaf* and *The Topiary Garden* are also available from Sceptre.

SCEPTRE